ALSO BY

SACHA NASPINI

Nives

OXYGEN

Sacha Naspini

OXYGEN

*Translated from the Italian
by Clarissa Botsford*

Europa
editions

11/6/21

Europa Editions
8 Blackstock Mews
London N4 2BT
www.europaeditions.co.uk

Copyright © 2019 by Edizioni e/o
First Publication 2021 by Europa Editions

Translation by Clarissa Botsford
Original title: *Ossigeno*
Translation copyright © 2021 by Europa Editions

A catalogue record for this title is available from the British Library
ISBN 978-1-78770-294-3

Naspini, Sacha
Oxygen

Printed ar

CONTENTS

OXYGEN

S heriff? John here."

"What's up, John?"

"I'm down at the Valley Elementary School."

"What? Graffiti again?"

"No. They're saying a kid has gone missing."

"Missing?"

"During recess. Back in class, the teacher said there was an empty desk."

" . . . "

"Sheriff?"

"Wait a minute, I'm thinking. I'll send Torczon and McClain out to patrol the area. If the kid is out of school, he can't be too far away. Have they called the parents?"

"George just asked the principal to call them."

"Okay. He'll be home by now, I bet."

"We'll keep looking around here."

"You know what kids are like."

"Not sure this time . . . George looks worried."

" . . . "

"Sheriff?"

"I'll let Chris know. You guys go ahead and walk the perimeter. I'm on my way."

THE STICK INSECT

They came to get him at eight P.M.

We'd been arguing because our upstairs neighbor had been down to complain that my music was too loud. There we were, sitting at the table in silence, the news blaring out of the TV. The same old duel to see who would cave in first and speak. It was never me. My father wasn't made for that kind of game. At some point, he'd come out with something stupid like, "We must remember to buy a lightbulb for the patio," as if he were picking up from where he'd left off. And then he would give me that hangdog look. If we ever kept it up past dinnertime, he would come and knock on my bedroom door with some lame excuse. I would stare at him as he stood there in his ratty old bathrobe; he just couldn't go to bed without saying goodnight first.

We were looking down into our plates, and his eyes kept flicking up at me, I could feel it. Then I scored yet another victory when he capitulated as usual with a pathetic, "Can you pass the salt, please?"

That was when they rang.

I went to get the door; the neighbor would have to deal with me this time. I yanked it open, and in front of me on the landing was a man with an office worker's haircut wearing a leather jacket. Standing behind him were some Carabinieri in uniform. That's what he said they were: "Carabinieri." He waved a piece of paper at me and mumbled something about a warrant.

"What?" I said, trying not to laugh in his face.

They marched in, pushing me to one side, flattening me against the wall. Within seconds, they had spread out into every room. Weapons drawn.

My father vanished into thin air. One second, he was cutting a slice of the onion frittata; the next, he was gone. In his place were a pack of Carabinieri pulling out drawers, ripping mattresses open, and tearing pictures and family photos out of their frames.

It was October 6, 2013. As everybody knows, that was the day Professor Carlo Maria Balestri was arrested on multiple counts of abduction, torture, murder, and concealing his victims' bodies. I was 27, he was 59. Suddenly I was alone in the world.

When I was a kid, I wanted to be a pilot. My father would often come home from his lectures with a gift for me to unwrap: a model aircraft kit. My prize planes are still lined up on the shelves in my room. There's a Corsair F4U-7, for example; as well as an LFG Roland C.II biplane, a Transall C-160, even a Concorde. My best model is the Red Baron's Fokker Triplane. In the evenings he would sit with me and help me pull all the little plastic parts off their molds. My father observed my excitement at the miniature details with benevolence. We had paintbrushes as thin as eyelashes that could reach into the tiniest corners. Styluses of all sizes, brushes, glues, paints, files, solvents . . . My father was obsessed with the minutiae. He didn't do anything; he just watched. In the lamplight, his eyes were like ice-blue asteroids looking down on my inexpert fumbling. I was always in a hurry to finish. Applying the decals was a nightmare, my fingers suddenly clumsy. Once I had glued the fuselage down, I rushed to stick the insignia on the wings. "Pity," he would mutter, imperturbable as ever, bemused when I stuck the transfers at the wrong angle and messed up the smooth plastic surface.

He kept the little girls in a shipping container.

Every summer, we used to rent an apartment at Capo Sant'Andrea for a two-week vacation with days at the beach and evening strolls. My mother would breathe a sigh of relief the moment we landed on the island. She would open up the big French windows and sit on the balcony for the first half hour, smoking and staring out at the horizon as the waves crashed against the lunar landscape of the rocks below.

I loved meeting up with the local kids. At the beginning, we were awkward, as if we needed to get to know one another again each time. Especially Angela. She changed every year, but that August of '98 she was totally transformed: her body, her behavior, her gaze, everything was different. We were both twelve, and there was something new in the air that put us on edge. Every afternoon, I left my parents under their beach umbrella and escaped to the little cove where the locals went. Marco had become my rival. Until the year before, we had been blood brothers; now, rather than playing, he challenged me at every turn. He never missed the chance to point out the pain in the ass we vacationers were: we loaded up our cars with everything we needed, even our own toilet paper, and came over to this paradise from the mainland bringing nothing but trouble.

The evening I had my first kiss, my bike got wrecked.

While I was showing off my high dives to my summer sweetheart, another little girl was locked up in a pitch-black cargo container. A furnace in that heat. A chain around her neck. An iron bed frame soldered to the floor, the stench of her own piss and shit. My father must have left enough supplies for her to survive the whole two weeks of our vacation; I wonder how he felt about that little gamble deep inside. She had been held there since March '93, around the time Amanda had disappeared. She was six at the time. The same age as me. When they searched our house in 2013, they found a lock of her hair in the pages of a book.

Angela and I used to write each other letters. In September, there was one a week. Then, as the months went by, there were fewer and fewer, until in June and July we were down to nothing. When August came around, the cycle would begin again.

We wrote stupid kids' stuff, pages of sweet nothings. I would sometimes open the envelope I had sealed the night before and copy out my letter one more time, being careful not to make too many promises. Other times, I regretted sending it the second I dropped it in the mailbox.

In February of '99, things changed. Rather than write about what me and my friends were up to, or how mean my teachers were being, something more urgent had come along. Something that shifted all my thirteen-year-old priorities. My Mom was sick. The light in our house was beginning to go out.

Angela was the only one I could talk to. She wrote long letters back, pages and pages of words, which I clung onto desperately. What I liked was that she never tried to reassure me. I had asked her not to tell her parents; we didn't need any more phone calls in the house, and I didn't want our correspondence to be poisoned by her mother's and father's words. We were still us; we wanted nothing to change. Except that now I was walking around with a knife in my heart. I wrote about my mother's medication, her pain, the doctors whose hourly fee cost my father one month's salary. Without ever talking about my Mom's illness, Angela was with me. She told me about her favorite singers, films she loved, books and graphic novels I should read, because they had changed her life. Sometimes, she would slip a photo into the envelope, either of herself or of a landscape, with a message written on the back.

I followed her suggestions faithfully. I bought CDs and 300-page books filled with dragons. I went to the movies on my own. Or I would stand by the window, where I could see the entire gulf, and gaze out at sea. From my bedroom on the sixth floor, there were evenings when Elba looked a stone's throw away, with the shadow of Corsica behind it. Angela was there, on the side of the island hidden from sight. I could see her anyway, trapped on that spit of land, like a princess in a tower waiting to be rescued. She may have been there at that very moment, writing to me. A racking cough from my parents' room would shake the walls and I would pick up my pen and start writing back.

In April, I was woken up in the middle of the night. I thought to myself, "Okay, I'm ready," though it turned out not to be what I'd expected. Mom, who was still able to stand back then, was at the door. She'd just called an ambulance.

My father was taken straight to the emergency room. He had a perforated appendix, bad enough to kill an elephant, with no warning signs and no apparent cause. His diet was monastic: he never used salt, and only ever ate light broths, vegetable soups, or white meat, with a drop of olive oil if he was in the mood for indulging—but that was rare. Wine was reserved for cooking, if that. The only treat he allowed himself was a pastry once a month; he couldn't resist the Sicilian cannoli they made at the bakery on via La Marmora. Cramming the thing into his mouth, he would say, "A *cannolo* a month takes the strife out of life."

It didn't seem serious at the time, but it almost did him in. It was a freak case: he went straight from the operating table into a coma for two days. After a spell in intensive care, they kept him in for ten more days to check on his progress, and allow him to regain his strength. I stuck close to Mom, who had enough problems of her own. The idea that I might be orphaned was killing her. But if he had died that night, it would have been better for all of us. My mother had gotten on the pay phone in the smokers' room, her husband's notebook in her hand. There were consequences: canceling his lectures meant classes to reschedule, courses to postpone, symposiums to defer, conference organizers to disturb. I watched the woman, reduced to skin and bones, busy herself. The task of rearranging Professor Balestri's calendar switched her light on again, almost like a cure.

What's more, I had tangible proof of my father's integrity and strength. He held the reins of our life, and never let go. He dealt with his wife's illness, the exhausting hospital routine, teaching, papers to write. Me. The repercussions of the forced break were palpable. It was during those days that I began to think of him as a kind of hero. Being a world-famous anthropologist was the least of it; it was the way he was so clear-headed, keeping up with everything. He lined up all his thoughts and proceeded with laser precision; there was never any energy wasted. He dominated his emotions. Kids at school thought being the son of an anthropologist must be boring as hell; fathers who could tune carburetors, or modify exhaust pipes to make their motorbikes go at a 100 mph, were preferable. Mine knew everything about humanity and its transformations. He could pick up any old knickknack and tell you the history of mankind. The shape of a goblet. The façade of a building. Anything set him off. I looked at him in his hospital bed, poised and unfailingly polite to the doctors and nurses. His main concern was to be presentable. After this unexpected stint away, I hate to think what he found when he went back to the container.

When the coffin went underground, a piece of me followed my mother down there. I felt a hand come and rip something out of me. All of a sudden, my legs caved in, and I fell on my ass on the gravel. But I refused to cry. It sucked having all those eyes on me; it was like being stared at with no clothes on. I ran away before they finished burying her. After saying goodbye to the few relatives and close friends we had, my father found me in the car with the radio on.

Another life started. Sumira, a Romanian housekeeper my father had taken on full-time, woke me up in the morning now. She was always chirpy, and sang relentlessly. I resented her at first: it felt like her life had been turned around by my mother's death. Then I got used to her, and we started talking. When she wasn't clucking like a hen, singing her little ditties, she would tell me all about her son, Vasile. His name sounded gross to me. According to her, he had a million talents. He was the best in everything, from high jump to piano. After a while, being compared all the time to this Vasile began to amuse me.

"Vasile tall six feet now," Sumira would say. "Vasile top of class for geography," "girl pull out hair when Vasile walk down street," she would boast. It became quite comforting.

The smell of the house changed. The whiff of watery Eastern European broths was so strong it caught in your throat all the way to the elevator. Some piece of animal was always simmering on the stove for hours. "Peasant cuisine," my father would say, with the enthusiasm of someone who was taking a journey through history rather than eating. I was given rice and boiled potatoes, served up on the same plate. While the other kids at school were fed spaghetti, I had to sit and eat Romanian grits or sour meatball soup. The stench clung to the walls. Going into the kitchen in the morning for my coffee made me gag, because the air was still thick with the stink of boiled meat. "Vasile eat pastrami to give him strong!"

I wrote to Angela about the madwoman in our house. She was amused; a few letters back and forth and Sumira soon become our favorite topic. I wrote about how much she liked her drink, and how we would die laughing when she was drunk. She was sometimes so tanked up that my father and I would have to carry her into the guest room. When we lifted her, she'd let out little sonorous farts. She snored so loudly that, on a few occasions, my father and I would find ourselves in the kitchen in the middle of the night like evacuees, our eyes bleary with sleep.

"Maybe we should go and check up on her," he would say, scratching his head, a little concerned because bringing down the ceiling like that snoring so loudly wasn't normal.

The following morning, Sumira would be in perfect shape, chirruping over the toast, her heavy body moving as deftly as a dragonfly.

"You have good night?"

She had fallen in love with our next-door neighbor, Corradi. A man with no pretensions, who had lived his whole life that way: with no pretensions. Anyone could see it in his face. A very old and infinitely kind widower, he had only one passion: 78 rpm records. His collection was boundless. Early in the morning, as I tried to down my caffè latte with a clothes-peg on my nose, he would drop the stylus on a Cetra Quartet record as soon as the breakfast news was over, and then he would carry on throughout the morning. I wrote to Angela about the doormat stakeouts and corridor greetings between this female giant and the mild accountant who had been retired for over a hundred years. They were sweet. They goaded one another with the tips of their swords, with old-fashioned courtesy. I tried to describe a feeling— that sometimes life lies in the little things, like saying good morning and good evening—but found only clumsy clichés. In the end, I erased everything.

Without Mom, there was no more Capo Sant'Andrea. Renting that house again would have been too painful, for many reasons. We spent the summer in town. My father spent most of it on his beach chair on the balcony, wearing the same old bathing costume. He always had a pile of books next to the lemonade that Sumira made in jugfuls, mostly for herself because she couldn't stand the heat. May to September for her were an apocalypse; all she did was fan herself with anything she could get her hands on. She was careful not to put so much as a toe in the sun; she would keep out of its way as if it were an insult. Worse, the devil itself.

I asked to go on a day trip to Elba on my own. I thought I was old enough. In any case, I wanted the challenge: getting the train all the way to Piombino and then an hour's ferry ride, followed by a bus from Portoferraio to Capo Sant'Andrea. (What my father didn't know was the rush of excitement I felt at the idea of surprising Angela.)

"No way."

That was his first reaction. Most kids would feel a spike of rage, but it was not like that for me. Since Mom had died, things were different. He was on my case now; thousands of anxieties had flared up in him all of a sudden. Maybe he felt he had to fill the gap his dead wife had left behind, or feared that my life was already on the brink of an abyss with no hope, which might one day drag me down. All this made him overprotective of me, and I was, ultimately, a willing victim. I was his priority: he was keen to declare it in every word and every gesture. Our team had lost a vital member. We bore the same wound. We shared the same pain, although from different points of view: this was the source of our strength.

But we were still two distinct people. We were careful to

avoid the mistake of entering the kind of room where echoing emptiness is transformed into an alliance that borders on morbidity. Or craziness We each needed our silence. We needed to turn our gaze back out onto the world, even though it had been occupied by a language of cruelty. In the end, I just said it. Straight and simple. My going away for a day might do him good, too. Checking up on one another was not a form of love. And, in any case, I wasn't contemplating a journey to another galaxy.

He took care of everything: tickets, times, strategies to adopt if there were any delays or missed connections. He explained his plan that evening at dinner. Sumira was singing under her breath as she rinsed the dishes.

At one point, she turned toward us and said, "Vasile do miles of journey every day in week, Krakow to Bucharest."

My father looked at her, annoyed.

"Please," he said. "We're talking about something important here."

Listening to him, anyone would have thought I was an explorer preparing for an expedition. I let him have his way on nearly everything, but the water cooler was too much. I stubbornly refused. He gave me money. Enough, probably, to book a return flight to New York.

"What if the sea gets rough?" he said, horrified. "What if you get stuck on the island? You'll have to rent a room . . . "

If there was anything I needed, anything, I should call. He had connections on the island: one call, and I would be rescued in an instant and taken to safety in some villa, where I should wait for new orders. Then he went to check the weather forecast.

It was a great trip, especially the ferry crossing. I stood out on deck the whole way, gazing at the coastline of the island. Being there meant so many things to me: I was moving forward despite the wild beast of grief biting at my heels. Mom was no longer with us, but here I was, sailing across this strip of sea, as I always had. Warmth coursed through my body in waves, surprising me with a hint of happiness. I was proud of myself for not just staying on my balcony to sunbathe. Even though it was only for a day, I was letting life follow the path that had been mapped out for me.

I stayed in this bubble of my own creation until I reached the bus stop that dropped me not far from our secret bay. I was even happy to be walking at the side of the road, under the hot sun, like a wandering traveler with a pack on his back, lost in the world. Then I made my way down to the beach.

Our meeting place had always been the same. My blood was at fever pitch. I had done little else but fantasize about my arrival on the scene. My favorite scenario envisaged Angela, sprawled on a towel, dozing after a swim, opening her eyes and finding me there, lying next to her. In her recent letters she had said desperately that August without me would be meaningless.

And yet, it seemed that she had found meaning in the blond guy she was coming out of the sea with. A guy I'd never seen before, maybe a foreign tourist. I was quite far away, sitting on one of those rocks that formed a crown, enclosing the bay and hiding it from the view of the hateful tourists on the main stretch of the beach. I observed the two of them just long enough to realize that my arrival on the scene would be embarrassing. My knees felt as wobbly as they'd felt the day Mom was buried. I would die of shame if I dropped on the ground like a wet rag and attracted unwanted attention. It was the right thing to think: adrenaline kept me on my feet. Anger did the rest.

I stumbled back on to the path; my head down. The sheet where my father had written all the bus and ferry times so scrupulously was already useless. I sat on the edge of the asphalt and did the last thing I would have imagined: I hitched a lift.

I was a clean-cut boy; nothing about my demeanor would have caused anyone to doubt my respectability. In fact, a car stopped almost immediately: a couple in their thirties, so full of life they made me want to throw myself off a cliff right there and then. The second I opened the door to get in, I heard a voice call, "Hey!" I turned and saw Marco, on his bike. I gave no sign I'd recognized him. I lowered my head and climbed into the car.

That was it, the escape I had dreamed of. At the Pier 3 kiosk, with a can of fizzy orange. The ferries came and went. In the end, I decided to change my ticket and go back to the mainland. My father would see I had come back early; I could already feel him, sniffing out my reasons. I would tell him in the briefest, most obscene, and most predictable manner possible—the manner of teenagers—that life is shit. And I would go to my room and reread Angela's most recent letters. Pages and pages, seas of words. After showing me a little affection last summer, she hadn't been in love with me for one minute. She had felt a duty to write because of what had happened to me. The discovery was a shock; it made my head spin.

On the return crossing, I went indoors and curled up on a seat with my Walkman plugged into my ears at full volume. This was what happened when you followed paths already trodden: it wasn't even midday, and I was retracing my steps with my tail between my legs.

At the port I had a stroke of luck, catching a connection at lightning speed. I staggered onto the train at the last possible minute, the doors closing on me, which led to a rebuke from the conductor because I hadn't had time to stamp my ticket. Forty minutes later, I was back at square one. Every face I saw on the station platform looked as if it was asking me whether I'd enjoyed my little adventure.

In the elevator, I breathed deeply several times, preparing myself mentally for the questions that would be fired at me as soon as I walked in the door. When Sumira saw me, her eyes opened wide.

"Already returning you are?"

I walked straight past her, hanging my head. I walked along the corridor and into the living room. The French windows were open wide to let in some fresh air, but there was no one on the balcony.

"Tata no home now," I heard Sumira say.

Tata. Try as I might, I couldn't get used to the way she called my father.

"Where is he, then?"

She opened her arms wide, theatrically.

Lucky for me, I thought. I went to my room and dumped my pack on the floor. I took my shoes off and looked at the stereo. What I wanted was a shield of sound to isolate me from the world. But next door, Corradi was already playing his 78 rpms, and it would have been rude to distort his music with a wall of my own noise. I threw myself on my bed, dressed as I was, with that music from another era playing in the background. Since I'd gotten up so early, and accumulated such a pile of shit over the day, I went out like a light.

When I woke up, it was evening. For a moment, I convinced myself it had all been a bad dream. I almost leaped out of bed, ready to go to Elba. But a second later, I was overwhelmed by the whole thing again. I looked at the time: I had slept more than five hours. My father had allowed me to rest. He must be here now, waiting anxiously to ask why I had come back so soon. The only way to get it over and done with as soon as possible was to deal with him head-on, without wasting another minute. There was only Sumira in the sitting room. She was airing herself on the sofa, her skirt lifted right up to her panties. For a moment I was hypnotized by the vision of white flesh, of the rolls that formed around her knees even when she was sitting.

"Isn't he back yet?"

She leaped to her feet, rearranging her skirt.

"Is there to be worried?"

The question sounded creepy, as if she were saying, "Is he dead?" Or, "Am I going to lose my job?"

"Has he called?" I asked.

Sumira shook her head. I looked at the clock again and had a sudden brainwave.

I ran into my room and put my shoes on. I grabbed the pack that I had left on the ground untouched and went back to the sitting room. Sumira hadn't moved an inch.

"You didn't see me, okay?"

She looked at me with the eyes of a dazed cow.

"Get it? I was never here today, okay?"

Eventually, she nodded, unconvinced.

"See you later," I said, hurtling toward the door.

If my plan hadn't worked out, I would have been in a heck of a lot of trouble. It would have been a real error to have bumped into my father right then. It was a good twenty minutes on foot from my house to the station; I was hell-bent on beating every record. I ran full throttle down through the underpass, even though there were no trains either coming or going. Once I was on the other side, I hid behind the column on platform 2 to catch my breath. Half an hour later, the train pulled in in perfect time. As the doors opened, and crowds of commuters and tourists poured out and crowded onto the stairs, I mingled in with them.

I saw my father on the other side of the exit barrier. He was standing outside his car, waiting. He waved as soon as he saw me.

I invented a fantastic day with my old vacation friends. I'd been having such a good time, I almost missed the bus for the port. He listened attentively without missing a syllable. At one point he said, "You haven't caught the sun at all," and I was sure he had found me out. I made a throwaway remark that I might have been out of the sun most of the day . . . with a forced smile to go with it. The idea that my father would imagine I had won the heart of the girl who had been writing to me every week was like twisting a knife in my gut.

During dinner, Sumira kept staring at me; she winked every time my father shifted his gaze away from me. I went on shoveling food into my mouth pretending to be hungry, while he continued with his allusive comments.

"You need to get your strength back!"

He exuded such pride at the idea that his son had made a conquest. I started to yawn and told him I was dog tired. Sumira, who had been lost in thought, turned around instinctively.

"How this possible?"

I stared her down.

But my father was distracted. He didn't hear a thing. I said goodnight and left the kitchen, praying that our loquacious housekeeper wouldn't get me into trouble.

It was August 12, '99. The same day that eight-year-old Laura had vanished into thin air. By the time she was rescued, she had turned 22.

A plot fifty miles from home, on the edge of a beech forest just outside the city. Far away from any cultivated land. A sturdy fence and a well-kept lawn. In the middle, a brick block: two rooms, a bathroom, and a kitchen. To the right, a wooden cabin cruiser, on a boat trailer with flat tires. The nearest settlement at least a ten-minute drive away, on a long dirt track. Behind the house, a container half-hidden by the boughs of an old willow. At first glance, it could have been a toolshed.

Angela went on sending me letters for a few weeks. I let

them pile up without opening them. Then she stopped. At Christmas, an unexpected letter arrived with little stars stuck all over it. I put that one in a drawer unopened, too.

Everyone remembers what they did on New Year's in the year 2000. My father and I went to the mountains for a few days. To spend some time together away from the frenzy of the festivities. We were identical that way: neither of us could stand large crowds and loud behavior. I was still a boy. I had just turned thirteen, but I could already sense how my nature had been molded by my father's perpetual brooding. We walked the same; we both had a shuffling gait, and often bumped into things for no reason. "Like father, like son," he would say, smiling. Nonetheless, we both liked walking. Just as we both liked the cold. When we were away together, he behaved more like a father. He shed the guise of the famous academic, courted by universities around the world. There was one thing that bound us in particular: our passion for the past. In those days, I could feel the spark inside me but couldn't give it a name. I would be enthralled by a centuries-old portal. I would stand there and stare, imagining all the lives of the people who had once walked through it. Who were they? What events did their lives initiate? How did they brush their teeth? I could sit on a bench in an old church for thirty minutes or more without doing anything. The silence. And the smell. The saints' feet, like polished gold after being stroked by countless devotees. I would add a caress of my own. I pictured all the hands that had rubbed the same spot before me. It was a game. I would imagine brushing against the hand of a washerwoman who had lived three hundred years ago, of a soldier leaving to fight a war, of a young woman who had come last Wednesday, already regretting betraying her newly-wedded husband . . . Like everyone else, I was the end result of infinite paths and accidents that had tilted the world one way rather than another. The evidence was everywhere: from the kind of jacket

I chose to wear to the algebra I employed to order my thoughts.

My father called it "wanderlust" and claimed few people experienced it. He said I was lucky, and I believed him, to a certain extent. He was never intrusive with me. If I had been crazy about becoming a professional soccer player, which is what all my boring friends wanted to be, he wouldn't have batted an eyelid. If anything, it was me badgering him. I would pick out some random object and ask him to tell me its history. It was quite an experience starting with the blades of a ceiling fan and being catapulted into the past. My father would recreate a timeline, drawing the invention of pencils, parabolic curves, and the Gregorian calendar into the story. A wild caper through the centuries, circling over wars and technological revolutions. Buffeted by the winds of change, I clung to the invisible thread that held everything together. As he spoke, I actually felt things move around inside me. I was like a satellite surveying world events at impossible speed, a decade a second. He usually ended his accounts with the words, "And here we are now." It was like coming down to earth, after a journey through the millennia. With a jolt, I realized I was back in my own shoes. Everything felt significant, even a crack in the wall of a café.

Another favorite topic was my grandparents, whom I'd never met. My father's face would light up on the subject. But I always had the sensation that there was a pin stuck in his throat when he said their names. Talking about them meant talking about himself. Talking about them meant talking about me.

He and I share a trademark that makes us unique and identifiable: the top joint of our pinkies is abnormally bent. "If you want to prove you're a Balestri, show them this," he would say, holding up his pinkie. I would stick mine out: they were exactly the same. We were cut from the same cloth. A single gene that continued to reproduce itself through the mists of time, surviving contamination, plague, and war. In the course of world history, there may have been buccaneers, gold diggers, Ancient Roman scullery boys, and cutthroats with the same feature. I was the most recent link in the chain. Blasting toward the future, I contained within me the mysteries of so many lives, from the most adventurous to the ones wasted. The way we sneeze. Our tics. Where did it all come from? Inside of me was a train that had been traveling since the beginning of time; listening to its rhythmic clickety-clack in my father was comforting. I guessed what he was doing with his deliberate, measured gestures. He was passing the baton. A mirror image gradually fading; a new one in the making for the future. A blade ripping through time. Our pinkies. Now, the ball was in my court. For most people, being told they are unique was a hackneyed line from a soap opera. For me, it was an echo of a distant thud. The breeze of my father's wander-lust ruffling my hair.

According to the investigators' reports, there were only three proven charges of kidnapping and murder they could indict my father on, but they suspect the actual figure is at least double that. Apart from Laura, none of the bodies have ever been found.

Laura looks normal when you see her. She's making an effort. She has a group of friends; she's trying hard in her stud-ies. She even has a boyfriend.

I sometimes spy on her in the reflection of a store window or bar mirror. She blanks out a lot. There are moments when her eyes look lost, her pupils dilate, and she descends into a well of blackness only she knows. She may be disoriented for whole minutes. Around her in the bar, the gang goes on chugging beers, the noise levels rise. They are all fired up with youth. The way they light their cigarettes is so stagey, it makes me want to wipe out the whole species. They are completely self-involved. They don't even notice that their friend has shut down, gone back to her iron box, and bolted herself in. I, too, have been locked there, looking for a ray of light, since October 2013. They could put their cigarettes out on the back of her hand, and she wouldn't blink. No expression of fear. Laura switches off; she erases herself. A pang of some kind suddenly courses through her and she goes into a kind of suspension. I'm the only one who recognizes her, who understands her. The day they freed her was the day they imprisoned me. Over the last five years, I have occasionally treated myself to this little vacation, despite the long drive and the expense. Laura was the breath of fresh air everyone said I needed. The oxygen of knowing I was not alone.

I knew her long before she was found: he used to call her name in his sleep. Sumira and I would run to his bedside in the middle of the night. He cried out so loudly that he woke her from her monstrous snores. His nightmares started after Mom died. We would find him sitting up in bed still asleep, lashing out with his arms. He would be talking, yelling at someone, or wheedling pathetically. "Are you cold?" he would ask, or, in floods of tears, say, "Sorry, I'm so sorry." My heart was rent twice over: first, because I had to see him in that state, and second, because I understood how hard it must have been to keep up his façade during the day. Worse, he gave voice to my own pain, which I hadn't yet learned to express. There were some mornings when I would open my eyes and for a second forget everything. Then came the hammer blow to the head: "Mom is dead." Other times, the realization landed out of the blue, while I was focusing on something else entirely, a jolt that made me spin out of control.

Sumira was always kind.

"You go bed. I think to your father."

I was happy to accept, because seeing my father in the grip of an episode like that paralyzed me; I would stand there uselessly, one foot out the door.

"I coming!" Sumira would shout. "I here!"

Her stocky legs pumped as if she were running a race. The following day, I would find her busying herself in the kitchen as if nothing had happened.

Reconstructing your entire life by putting together hidden clues left by a sick father is not easy. At the beginning I looked for the pieces of the puzzle; part of me was unable to control my impulse. I tried to crack the code in all our Christmases and Easters, or the day he finally gave in, after months of my pestering, and we went together to buy my first scooter. I searched for signs in my choice of high school, when I ended up in the traditional classics school rather than the art academy, which was my burning ambition at the time. I examined every day of my life, whatever the weather, every boring afternoon. All those years there had been a black river flowing right under us. The only relief was that at least Mom had been spared.

In his nightmares, my father called out to her. One night, though, his ravings were more distinct. One phrase in particular planted a seed of doubt. "I need to clean you." When Mom was ill, he had never had to clean her. There was always someone else to do the job. When Sumira saw my shock, she suggested as usual that I go back to my room.

"You no listen him."

After October 2013, revisiting the scene in a different light was strange. My father was being devoured by the dreadful foreboding of the dead, perhaps. The spirits are always there, somewhere. Muzzled creatures with big eyes. They see everything. They scour your conscience. Even your dreams.

If on that August day in '99 I hadn't insisted on an impromptu trip to surprise a young girl on Elba, things would have been very different for Laura. I keep telling myself that another little girl would have taken her place, sooner or later. But for Laura, it was as if my longing for a summer kiss, and my urge to feel alive after Mom's funeral, had somehow led to her being chosen. Therapy hasn't helped at all. The years go by, and the nagging thought is still there, like a worm. When it gets bad, I need to pack in a hurry and choke down the 250 miles in silence. I need to make sure she's okay, and I need to know I'm not the only one carrying the stench of a container around with me.

Laura even talked to me once.

I realized that I was tailing her too obviously, and hadn't taken the usual precautions. Early morning. I was walking ten steps behind her in the bustle of the city. Midwinter, iced-over puddles, and piles of dirty snow on the sides of the road. It was a route we had taken together many times, unbeknownst to her.

Normally, I hang back at the lights and step off the sidewalk on the corner, as if I'm about to hail a cab. Once the light is green, I set off on her tail again. This time, though, I needed something more. It happens. To assuage my pain, I need to get closer to her life. I'll do anything, even collect the cigarette butts she drops on the road. If they haven't fallen into the dirt, I pick them up and smoke the last few puffs until the filter starts to burn. Or I may see her throw something in the bin: some chewing gum paper (Laura prefers the Brooklyn brand, spearmint flavor), or a subway ticket. If I'm lucky, I manage to salvage a movie ticket stub, or an exhibition entry ticket. They are good omens, for me. They show that Laura is trying; she is living. Catching a glimpse of her singing at a concert moves me to tears. Talking to her would be totally against the rules. In cases like my father's, there are strict boundaries to respect. I would probably get into trouble walking on the opposite side of town without notifying the proper authorities.

That morning I was hungry for news. I followed her, registering every move. It looked like she was late and in a bad mood. She was rummaging desperately in her bag. She may have been looking for her cigarettes (Laura prefers Camel Lights, the blue pack), or maybe her wallet.

In her confusion, she drops a bunch of keys. I'm right behind her, literally shadowing her. She stops, turns, and retraces her steps. We're standing there, facing one another. I bend down and pick up the bunch. I hand it to her.

"Thank you," she says, a wan smile on her lips, her head miles away.

Laura's eyes are green. She turns around and carries on down the road. Leaving me in the middle of the crowded street, motionless.

Laura locks herself into toilets in cafés or bars. Mostly in the afternoons, when she plunges into the city alone. She takes the first train that pulls into the subway station, and lets herself be dragged out to sea. Sometimes I lose her. Other times I don't. I prize the automatic doors open and jump in, taking up my position behind someone or other, so I can keep an eye on her, especially as we approach a station. I follow her on the escalators, along the sidewalks. In all weather. Until she ducks into a café for no apparent reason.

The first few times, I waited outside. Every minute that went by, I was stabbed by the thought that she had seen me. That she must have slipped out of some back entrance. I could see the police car in my mind's eye. Then, I started following her inside.

Laura is looking for a cage. The impulse comes out of the blue, and she is consumed by it. She can't control it. One second, she is walking along the road perfectly happily; the next, she is holed up in the john, locking both doors behind her. I go in and order a drink at the counter. There are times when there are so few people that we are the only ones in the place, aside from the barman, who is always either half asleep or with one eye on a TV hanging up in a corner somewhere. The scene is bizarre: me on the outside, her on the inside. She seems to want it that way.

I want it that way, too. I am in thrall to the agony of it. Every minute that goes by, the risk that she comes out and finds me there increases. She has no idea what the son of the psychopath who kept her locked up for years looks like. She may not even know he had a son. Since I cannot afford to allow anything about me to attract her attention, I generally wrap up well before I start stalking her. If there are a lot of people, I can hide in the crowd. When we are alone, every tick of the clock is quicksilver coursing through my body.

A quarter of an hour. Twenty minutes . . . I'm usually the first to cave in: I leave a couple of bills on the counter and I run outside, where there's a little air. I find a good place to watch the door. Laura often comes out much later; meanwhile, I have turned into a block of ice. I wonder: Who is stalking whom? Who is imprisoning whom?

Other times, someone in the bar notices. The bathroom has been locked for over an hour. Should we call an ambulance? In that case, I quietly slip off the bar stool, not even daring to take my wallet out, in case it creates a stir.

I can't tell my therapist any of this. Naima is convinced I've made huge progress. Most people in my position, she says, would have gone to the dogs a while back. She's in a class of her own in treating posttraumatic stress disorders. In my case, this means rebuilding the foundations of my existence. Naima calls it "cognitive restructuring." In the early days, she would ask me to frame my father's arrest as a terrible car accident I had somehow crawled out of alive and, most importantly, without any responsibility for what had happened.

Another point she always makes is that after the events in 2013 it is as if my father were dead. The fact that he's rotting in jail shouldn't muddy the picture. He no longer exists. The man who gave me life, who had been with me since the day I was born, was relegated to the past. What we have to do, Naima says, is *restore natural information-processing in the elements present in my memory, in order to achieve an adaptive resolution and forge new associative links.* That's what EMDR therapy dictates. I say to Naima, "We're the same blood." She says, "That's another matter."

Essentially, what I'm being asked to do is burn the centuries-old bridge behind me. I no longer have a "before." The tar has melted, the road that leads back into the past, and links my history to everything else, has a crater in it. My father. The man who molded me, taught me, protected me, advised me, guided me, dressed me. The man who loved me. My father is not just some accident that happened to me. My pinkie speaks loud and clear.

The truth is that I'm in denial about what he did. I don't tell Naima this; it would be a waste of a session. He may have been coerced. He may not have had a choice. There might have been some kind of confraternity engaging in sadistic ancient rituals. We all know scientists can be pretty weird. In Eastern Europe, some big shots with deep pockets had set up a lucrative business procuring kids, who were then killed, just to see what happened. Could Mom have been involved somehow? I went as far as making up a possible explanation: maybe she gave birth to a little girl before she had me. The girl died young in some tragedy, so my mother forced her husband to abduct other little girls to keep them safe, like dolls. After thinking these thoughts, I find myself in the bathroom vomiting. In order to clear one parent, I'm smearing both.

My father isn't talking. He has never talked. Ever since his arrest, he's declared his innocence, despite the evidence against him. He had preserved a lock of Amanda's hair in a book. He had kept a milk tooth from the little girl before Amanda for years in a little drawer of a jewelry box that he'd bought in Tibet before I was born. Her name was Sara. When I was a kid, I used to play with that little front tooth. "It's yours," he would quip. "Time certainly does fly . . . " Mom was duped, too. She thought it was endearing that he had held on to that trophy of my childhood. Sometimes, when I was fooling around, I would put it in my mouth, right in front of my big new teeth.

My relics are something else: garbage. If I were braver, I'd go through her bins, but it would be too risky. Laura loves rock music. Her favorite colors are black, purple, and blue. She likes writing. While she's riding the subway, she's mostly writing in her notebook, her buds stuck deep into her ears like me on the crossing back from Elba.

There are moments when I'd like to drop my mask. I fantasize about going up and asking her point blank, "What was it like? What did he talk to you about? Was he kind, at least?"

If from the investigation, her direct testimony, and the trial proceedings, it had ever transpired that he had touched her, I think I would have killed myself. When I say this to Naima, she looks at me with a critical frown. "You still feel responsible," she says. It's not like that. What I continue to feel is that I am fading, as if what gave life to me had been a hallucination. Laura had not accused my father of sexual abuse of any kind. At the end of the day, this was the only extenuating circumstance. It's something, at least. I'll take whatever I can get.

The fact that she had categorically refused a million-dollar offer to serialize her story created a sensation in the news. A book. A film. The kind of people who feed on TV railed against her for weeks. What an idiot. She'd been held for fourteen years; the least she deserved was a rich payout. Everybody wanted to know her name. See her face. There were some who had imagined she would be on all the afternoon shows and complained her appearances were too fleeting; others wanted her to run for elected office. Some people achieve the most incredible heights of obscenity. Spoken by the son of a psychopath, this may sound bizarre.

Spoken by the son of a psychopath, everything sounds bizarre. Whatever you do, you're doomed. People in town suspect the same poison runs in my blood—a drop of it, at least. I agree. And I pay the consequences.

At 32, I don't have a girlfriend. The few relatives I had have vanished; same with my friends, including the ones I'd had the longest. Each in their own way, they hung on tooth and nail for as long as they could. But they didn't make it. Nobody has made it with me. Because it's too much. I can't expect anyone else to shoulder the burden of my daily torture. Inviting me to a Christmas dinner triggers unpredictable forces that end up ruining the party for everybody. The point is not so much that my father is my father. The point is that I am his son.

But I don't jump ship, even though Naima is not completely against the idea of resetting my life, getting a new name. It would be a significant move, with outcomes that, day by day, might have a *positive impact on my cognitive framework*.

Sometimes I fantasize about it. I pick a name, like Piero Berti for example, and ask myself, Do I look like a Piero Berti? Or a Saverio Marchi, maybe? I experiment with more exotic possibilities . . . Given the uniqueness of my case, I don't think the courts would kick up a fuss. In the paper, I read about people who have suffered tragedies and, for a moment, I try on their names as if they were a new jacket. How does it fit? It's a hard exercise, even if it's just in my mind. How would I feel as Filippo? What about Giovanni? Or Peter? Asking me to reinvent my life like this, at my age, is unfair. Naima is upbeat about it. Of course she is: at the end of the session she gets to be herself still. I say it aloud, with a shudder, "If I woke up tomorrow as an Andrea, everything might be different." Her reply is always the same, "Would it really be so bad?"

For people who don't know me, it wouldn't make any difference. I could call myself a Wi-Fi password, upper- and lower-case letters included. But try telling that to the 20,000 souls living in my little town. They all know who I am, where I come from. I was born and raised in the bosom of the devil. They are unable to separate my father from me. I should know; I have the same problem. It's an impossible task, because my identity is not only what I perceive, it is also what other people perceive. I'm embroiled in the story. The primordial soup that spontaneously generated me in September '86 is still warm. Resetting a name means resetting a whole life. The first step would be to leave town. If you want a fresh start and a new ID you need to break with your past, or it's all a joke. You need to vanish into thin air, so that nobody can contradict you. Or recognize you.

The article says 562 people have disappeared since the beginning of the year. In addition to the 52,990 people who vanished without a trace between January 1974 and December 2017. At least the story of three little girls has been reconstructed.

Laura is still proudly Laura. The first time I saw her in a photo, the investigators were trying to establish once and for all that I wasn't involved in the kidnapping, and that I knew absolutely nothing about it. I stared at her face for a long time, deaf to their questions. The trauma was still fresh; I was munching sedatives like candy. I sat there, gazing into the eyes of a girl who was just a few years younger than me. What winded me was that suggestion of a smile: a shadow that made a tiny pucker in her lips. It looked like she was posing for a passport photo. Sitting beside me was Martini, our family attorney, who had known me forever. After the umpteenth unanswered question, right about when he was saying, "Ladies and gentlemen, I think my client is . . . " I fainted on the spot.

Mr. Martini was the one who kept me up to date on the investigation. "Don't read the papers," he said. "Forget about TV." I couldn't blast myself to the other side of the earth: my witness statements were vital in investigating new leads, providing tips for some line of inquiry or other. I didn't attend the trial. The last thing I needed was for my face to be plastered all over the gossip magazines. Closing all my social media accounts was the first thing I had to do in order not to be crushed. Mostly, though, I couldn't bear the idea of seeing him. My father. I pictured him in the dock, like the hired killer of a mafia boss.

In the meantime, the property and land he had secretly owned for decades had been combed for evidence. There was nothing. Not one hair. Given the other physical evidence, however, it was not easy for Martini to enter an insanity plea. It was unlikely to be accepted in a man who had given a lecture to several hundred people two days before his arrest, entitled "Notions of Biopower, Naked Life, and the State of Exception." It was during one of our debriefings with my attorney that I found out what the girl in the photo was called.

I was going out with Elisa at the time. After going steady for a year, we had been planning to take the plunge: she wanted to introduce me to her parents. Well, that didn't happen.

I was truly in love with her. If things had gone differently, we may have had our first child by now. We used to play around with different names; I liked Alvise because there was no St. Alvise in the calendar. She laughed. She wouldn't have let me ruin a kid's life, with no saint's day to celebrate—even under torture. So, I explained its etymology: it was a doublet of the Germanic *Hlodwig*, which meant glory in battle. By that point, Elisa had started yawning.

I miss that child. I often think about him, until a red-hot blade slices through me, from my throat down to my heart. My father had kidnapped him, too. He had picked him up and hurled him into the perpetual darkness of a big box: that of unfulfilled promises. The feeling of nostalgia for a child that was never even born sits heavily in your stomach. In my imagination, he is two or three, barefoot and naked except for a pair of denim overalls. It's summer; we're in a field somewhere. Alvise has his mother's eyes and blond hair. His silent shriek as he calls out to me has the power to crack glass. Naima prescribes yet another cycle of drugs. At least I get a little sleep.

In the beginning, having Elisa was important. I was walking around with my guts in my hands. She didn't know what to say; she was as shocked as I was. She would cuddle up against me and say, "You need to react." That was the best she could do. I could read it in her eyes and hear it in her voice. She didn't believe it, either. Every time I realized there was no way out for me, it was like stepping into a dark place over and over again.

I wish at least Sumira had been there, with her out-of-this-world air and her crazy comments. When she needed to be, she had actually been quite sensible and firm. She had left us at least ten years earlier, once she had paid for Vasile's school, and set aside a nest egg for her future. Romania had changed in the meantime. I imagined her safely ensconced in some corner of Wallachia, and prayed she would stay there. She was enjoying the fruits of her labor; her whole life had been devoted to providing for her son and her family. But Martini told me they had interviewed her, too. I wonder how she reacted to the news that she'd been living in the house of a psychopath. She had cooked for him and ironed his shirts. Maybe she's the one waking up in the night screaming now.

The whole building was paralyzed by the news. Around town, there was little talk of anything else. A seaside town that filled up in the summer and emptied out in the winter was all of a sudden besieged by live satellite TV trucks. In the very early days, text messages from my close friends flooded in; they were duty-bound to write that they felt for me. Not one of them bothered to come and ring my doorbell.

The local dailies and TV stations had fresh meat to get their teeth into, for once. Their reports flashed over the national papers, beamed out of state news channels, and finally appeared overseas, too. The headlines echoed across the country: "Monster of the Gulf Arrested." I locked myself in my house, on my attorney's advice. I let the phone ring for hours. Elisa hung in there for a bit, but after two weeks she was worn out. She couldn't bring herself to touch me. She was exhausted by the avalanche of attention, most devastatingly from the townspeople: she was the girlfriend of that man's son. She started looking at me differently, as if the events had lifted a veil: there was something wrong with my profile, my gaze, my skinny body. I had followed in my father's footsteps academically, too. I had been making good progress, showcasing my qualities, and gradually convincing envious colleagues that nepotism had never played a role in my career. I'd persuaded them by dint of hard work and tangible results. It was easy, though, to see how I could have been seen as a clone, a more recent version of him. I had even developed a receding hairline, just like his.

Elisa knew him well. She had a thing about Mexican food

and had tried out a few recipes on us at home while the eminent professor, Carlo Maria Balestri, who knew everything about everything—including the origins of the Mesoamerican dishes—gave his usual running commentary. Discovering that there was a furious beast lurking beneath this diminutive man's gentle and benevolent exterior had shocked her to the quick. It had also unintentionally sparked the same doubt in her as in everyone else: was I a culture for the same germ? It's not something you can easily ask someone you're supposed to be building your future and having a child with. Until a couple of weeks before, she had thought the abnormal pinkie story was adorable. Now, she saw it as the mark of the devil.

She told me in tears: she'd had enough. She couldn't put her nose outside the door without people looking her up and down, avoiding her. Those that did say hello to her whispered things to one another as soon as she turned her back. I had been keeping away from the TV programs and full-page newspaper articles, but she forced them all down. It was too big a story. The whole town would take at least ten years to get over being known as the home of the "monster of the gulf," rather than for its white beaches and turquoise sea. Elisa kept saying she was sorry, though her sobbing made it hard for her to speak. She had to save herself. She was the first person to jolt me into thinking about the situation in a different way when she said, "I'll end up being the one locked up in that place."

Matteo Lorenzi was my best friend in high school. We shared a passion for action figures. He was in a class of his own, sculpting miniatures. He had started as a child, and by the age of 17 he was a champion modelist. He had a workshop in his bedroom, with a countertop that was incomparably better equipped than the corner of my desk where I still assembled model airplanes—though I was beginning to move more in the direction of spaceships. Matteo Lorenzi's room looked like an artist's studio. I was in awe of all his tools, micro-utensils of all shapes and sizes: drills, mini-lathes, clamps, Vernier calipers, even a blowtorch. Sheets of millimeter-squared paper everywhere, filled with freehand sketches. When he was making models, he would use special glasses that had an extra arm with a magnifying glass on it. Sitting at his workbench, he would pull a pair of surgical gloves out of a box, as if he were about to perform open-heart surgery. His face would become incredibly serious. And he would stop talking.

I loved watching him. He would sit there, hunched over his worktop, with a lump of putty on the back of one hand, which he would pick at with a hook. Then he would slowly flesh out a skeleton of steel wire built onto a champagne cork base. Every now and again, he would look up at a poster opposite his workbench filled with illustrations of the human body: men, women, fat people, old people, hands, clavicles, eye bulbs . . . He had tiny palettes filled with the material to fortify a hip, here; a folding drape of a soldier's armor, there.

It was slow work, which required the greatest concentration. Anyone else would have died of boredom sitting there doing nothing. But it gave me peace. All of a sudden, nothing else existed. The only thing that mattered was ensuring that Marco completed that miniature ogre successfully, with its little cyborg pirate boots, and one eye stuck right in the middle of its head. Two regiments of characters: Good and Evil. The good regiment was a phalanx of fantasy creatures with steel clubs, energy shields, and laser cannons mounted on their shoulders. The evil gang were aliens. A band of mutant brutes, some of whom looked like reptiles, others like big snails, or spiders with fire-spitting carapaces. All his creations were lined up along the walls, in glass museum-like cases. Every character had a corresponding index card: role, specialty, weapon, weakest link . . . a hint of its history and background, its origins. All these were filed in an album my friend let me leaf through, as long as I washed my hands first. The miniatures conscripted in each of the two armies had been photographed *en face*, in profile, in a three-quarter pose, and from behind. There were already a great number of them.

What was missing was the overall story. We talked about this a lot. Matteo hadn't even decided on a name for the respective armies, or the planet they were living on. He would always say, "I'll study the characters, then we'll see." He had started modeling at seven. At times he would pick one of his early creations out of the line and start building it over from scratch, bringing it up to the same level as the others. In the late afternoons, my friend would sometimes ask for help, and together we would envision new warriors. I was good at inventing names. I was particularly proud of one I came up with to dub the captain of the rebel fleet's aide-de-camp: Jason Wood. He was a soldier of fortune, with a robotic limb that was so powerful it could pulverize mountains. For now, he was still in the design stage on graph paper. When I came up with the name, Matteo's eyes lit up. It was essential to give a fighter an identity. In his mind, the putty was coming to life.

Needless to say, he won countless medals in competitions; all he needed to do was send in a Polaroid. He never displayed his trophies. He kept his cups and plaques in the back of his wardrobe. There was a whole world out there: guys who would spend a fortune to get their hands on a two-and-a-half-inch Superman sculpted by a well-known name in the field. Which is what Matteo Lorenzi was gradually becoming, despite his age and his constant fights with his mother. Until recently, she was dead set against her son's passion for "toy soldiers." Birthdays and Christmases were always the same. He never wanted money, or clothes, or even a scooter; just tools, materials, and anatomy books. Then, after he received the prize money, her ears pricked up. How could a tiny object like that sell for a month's salary? Matteo laughed in her face. In

America and Japan, there were people who could buy themselves houses with these things. His father said nothing. Because he wasn't there. He'd killed himself when Matteo was twelve.

I never asked him, and Matteo never talked about it. Everyone in the town knew: one morning, Lorenzi Sr. had not turned up to work. His engineer colleagues found him that afternoon hanging in the pine grove near the pier.

I spoke to my father about it often. The question that haunted me was simply, Why? His death left a window wide open onto darkness. The man had had a son, a wife, a home, a good job. And yet he had wanted to leave everything behind, as if what he had built up in his lifetime was worthless. He hadn't had a terminal disease; there was no shadow of a loan shark. Riccardo Lorenzi had killed himself, and that was that. My father would look into space, speechless. Then he would sigh deeply and say, "Look after your friend. Why don't we invite him to dinner one evening? What do you think?"

Matteo was no different from the others. He had the same issues and crushes as every other teenager. Who knows what was festering under his apparent normality? Perhaps making armies of monsters and warriors helped him clarify matters inside of himself: Good and Evil. He recreated the endless struggle between two different worlds in putty, giving every figure a form, a name, and a role. And then putting them all into a glass case.

I started making miniatures, too. Greek and Latin homework was a ready excuse to go over to Matteo's house, where I could devote myself to the hobby. "You're crap at this," he would comment, looking at my abominations. But I had fallen in love with the silent, intimate dimension of the activity. I abandoned my half-gutted Revell model parts in their boxes, and started relentlessly sculpting one-of-a-kind creatures with my hands. If a bomb had fallen outside my window, I would have had to complete the space buccaneer's eye patch before running to safety. The twists of steel wire had slowly given it a form, however crooked. It was my little monster. A creature that lived within me. I was just like him. Over time, I grew fond of my clumsily-proportioned miniatures. Even after I had painted them patchily, with their rough surfaces and sloppy features, they were a reflection of me.

(Happily, Matteo Lorenzi is now the senior modeling artist at a large Los Angeles animation studio. At a certain point in the story, his armies of Good and Evil were bought in order to create a videogame. Today, those characters, salvaged from the agony of abandonment or rejection, populate the afternoons of millions of kids. They are the allies of the acne-stricken across continents. Their passion. Their salvation, perhaps.)

Elisa left me, and I started sculpting Laura. Outside, the storms were still raging around the monster of the gulf, while inside I made miniatures of her face. The face in the photo. I covered a cranium the size of a thumbnail with putty, trying to find a resemblance. My only clue was memory, which was hazy after my blackout. Several times I got it so wrong that I found myself with the head of a dumb baby doll in my hands. Other times, I produced a complete stranger, who may well exist somewhere or other: a kindergarten teacher in Bundaberg, Australia, perhaps. Every now and again I would capture a feature: a cheekbone, for example. Or a hint of a hint of her puckered-lip smile that had struck me so much that day. There were also times when I gave myself the creeps: Was I just like the man who had kept her locked up? Was I looking for a little plaything to take care of? In these moments, I would scrape all the putty off again, right down to her skull. And I would ask for forgiveness. This was when Martini suggested I contact Naima.

She's happy today. She says my decision is a big step forward. "A new name is a new story," she says. I may be remodeling myself with a brand-new ID card, but the twists of wire at my core are the same. "It'll pass," she says. I must be patient; I must wait until the putty hardens.

For people in the town nothing has changed. Luca Balestri is the same as ever. Apart from the Carabinieri, nobody knows I'm getting a new driver's license with a different name on it. That I am now someone else.

Sometimes I need company, so I read profiles of the worst criminals. There are psychopaths who have killed more than 190 people. They are mostly stories of violence, but I gloss over that. I'm looking for other details. A quick Internet search reveals just how many archives there are out there. For every criminal there's the date of birth, height and weight, method, confirmed victims, place of imprisonment. Whether they have any children. This gives me pause. Children are rarely mentioned. Perhaps only when they have ridden the wave of macabre notoriety with books, interviews, and TV appearances. The general public is keen to hear what it's like living under the same roof as a killer. It's stuff that sells. Mostly, though, they stay in the background, licking their wounds. Raking in a little money with fifteen minutes of fame on a talk show is just not worth it. Putting your DNA on show doesn't have a price tag. The same is true for victims. You can count the ones who got out alive and exhibited themselves on the fingers of one hand. Most pick up the pieces of their lives and attempt to put them together again, in silence.

The things that still shock me about Laura are her cigarettes, and the way she uses her iPhone. She was a child when she was abducted: the Internet wasn't around yet. Her life had been put on hold for fourteen years. In the meantime, the world had made giant leaps forward. And yet, if you look at her on the street, she doesn't appear to have missed a thing.

The boy she's been going out with for a few months looks okay. He's an architecture student. He works three evening shifts a week in a restaurant. They don't seem to do anything special: they go for walks, eat out, go to the movies, or occasionally catch a concert with friends. Then they go up to his place. That's when I give up.

On my eighteenth birthday, I received an unexpected gift: the deed to the apartment. I leafed through the papers but didn't understand what they were for. My father chortled.

"So? Aren't you going to say anything?"

What was I supposed to say? He had given me official ownership of the apartment where I had always lived (which I would have inherited anyway, at some point). It didn't feel like such a great gift. I thanked him, but a certain disappointment must have been legible on my face. He went on chuckling; he was giddy. Then he said, "Whatever happens, nobody will ever be able to take these four walls away from you." I looked askance at him. Who would ever want to do anything as mean as that? Then, no longer able to contain himself, he pulled a key fob out of his pocket. It had a Peugeot symbol on it.

"It's yours," he said. "But don't make me sick with nerves."

We hardly ever spoke about money; it made him go into a weird place in his mind. It may have been a form of embarrassment. I knew for sure that, though we were not filthy rich, we were definitely on the wealthy side. Every year, after the reading lists for his courses came out, his books sold like hotcakes. Titles such as *The Anthropology of Landscape, Education for Diversity: Intercultural Studies,* and *Family Forms and Gender Relations* were just a few of the best-sellers, the royalties of which—in addition to his salary as a full college professor, conference fees, and TV guest appearances—fleshed out his bank account. His sales in that segment of the market had been good for years, and publishers in the field courted him. Balestri was a name that guaranteed top-notch figures. A cutthroat auction was held for the rights of *Material and Immaterial Culture*. We didn't even celebrate when he finally signed the contract, but when Martini showed me his savings, I couldn't believe my eyes.

I sometimes wonder about them: all those students. He penetrated their lives, opened new horizons to them. That man with the gaze of a dreamer, with seemingly no desire to feed his own ego, nurtured the minds of the new generations. He shed light on countless objects using nothing but his own illumination. These students keep me company, too. Troops of young people marching toward their future, with fire in their veins. Steaming vats that Professor Balestri filled with soup and stirred. What must it have been like for them to discover that globules of venom had been floating in there too? Did they feel contaminated?

Today, Professor Balestri's books are all out of print. However, there is a flourishing secondhand market for the titles among those who consider them satanic relics, and those who continue to defend his work, which has been recognized by the scientific community the world over as still relevant. The debate is ongoing: the morality that devours a genius. People said things like, "Hitler may have baked wonderful cakes," followed immediately by responses such as: "If only his mother had baked one that evening instead of pulling down her panties." If only.

When I'm not too worried about Laura, I go and do some quick grocery shopping and then drive for forty minutes. I turn off the provincial road and drive up the dirt track to where the wood starts getting thicker.

It's all my property now. At first, I ignored that plot, the monster's cave. And yet, I was fatally attracted to it. One day I made up my mind. Two years had already gone by since everything happened. It hurt, but I had to see the spot where my father had spent so much time. See who he was in that crease of his existence. The details would help me understand. I wanted to make sure I'd really had nothing to do with it all.

I came upon a wall of overgrown grass with an ordinary-looking little house in the middle. The willow tree had grown, its branches twisting into the wild thorn bushes that had grafted themselves onto it. On the right were the remnants of a boat, the prow upended as if it were about to vanish into the waves: a picture postcard from the bayou.

Miraculously, what was left of the seals on the gate had resisted. The rust-corroded chain slid off as I shoved the gate with my shoulders. I knew that I would be entering a dark kingdom once I crossed that threshold. I crossed it anyway.

The first time I stayed ten minutes at most. All I did was walk around the perimeter fence, where some plum trees had grown spontaneously. There was wheatgrass everywhere. A feeble wind ruffled the willow, making it look like the head of a giant. The rustling of the leaves rose and fell in chorus, like waves. I sized up the brick house from where I stood: the windows were locked, the weather-beaten slats of the wooden shutters decaying. The plaster had started to crack. There was a loud clang as a gust of wind blew the gate shut. A thousand pins pricked my skin. A few paces further on, I could see the side of the house. And one end of the container.

We faced each other off for a while. The container was there, silhouetted against the tree, almost entirely hidden by thorns and branches, which were wrapping it in an embrace. A shudder ran through me; my instinct was telling me that, in order to free myself, I would have to open that iron mouth. But I couldn't. Seconds later I was in the car, my heart thumping.

I jerked it into first gear and screeched off, leaving a cloud of dust in my wake.

The Carabinieri had despaired. Who had transported the shipping container to that spot? And when? Had there ever been an accomplice? Their questions had remained unanswered. The fact that nobody lived anywhere near hadn't helped matters. The deed showed my father had owned the plot since February '79. I was born seven and a half years later. A routine application to the land registry to build the house and connect to local services had turned up. He had done everything by the book.

There is no point in trying to put the property on the market. Even without its connection to the monster of the gulf, nobody would want a place so far off the beaten track. The same goes for the apartment I pre-inherited on my eighteenth birthday. Not just the apartment, but the whole building is contaminated; maybe even the next one along. There's no clean air to breathe until you get to the end of the street. Some people still have their mortgages to pay off, and now they're trapped in a building with zero market value. And yet, the monthly mortgage payments are the same. Rumors abound. There are people who swear they can hear a little girl crying in the stairwell. It might have been the daughter of the couple on the first floor having a tantrum. Her name is Matilda. They torment her at school with the stories, and she lies in bed at night, eyes wide open, without realizing she herself is the ghost that's stealing her sleep.

This is what it's like: storm clouds roll across the sky, looking as though they may abate, but they never do. Old people, afraid of being home alone, are glued to the phone. Deliverymen shudder as they hold the front door open with one foot, and stick the mail into the letter boxes as fast as they can.

Cleaning up the plot was like sculpting a figure in reverse: I wasn't adding putty; I was taking it away. I filled bags and bags with garden waste and dragged them to the recycling plant. They looked like corpses wrapped in heavy black plastic. The little garden, as it had been left by the Carabinieri after they were finished digging, was slowly revealed: a slab of Swiss cheese full of holes and piles of earth. At one point I found a 100 lire coin dating back to 1983.

My early efforts were all directed at clearing the ground. The hard part would be when I started to tackle the house, and then the container. I kept my head down and slashed at tufts of overgrown weeds. Every now and then my scythe would clash against the iron. A metallic echo. What if someone answered from inside?

Dealing with the boat also gave me the creeps. One of the theories put forward during the investigation was that my father had used it to get rid of the little girls' bodies. The girls who hadn't made it; the ones before Laura. The cabin cruiser was legally registered. The police even uncovered a boating license.

The day I decided to open the door of the house I'd had to psych myself up on the drive over there; no wavering, I'd told myself, just stick the key in the lock and turn. My mind had manufactured an image that terrified me; setting foot inside there would be like walking into the monster's mouth. The container was its stomach.

I clung to my determination right to the last. The key was engaged, and I was all set to unlock the door with one terse twist of the wrist, but the deadbolt defeated my resolve. I almost snapped the key with my efforts, and scraped the knuckle of my index finger while I was at it. My interpretation of the situation was the only one possible: the derelict house was rejecting me. The energy flowing through me was saying:

don't do this, get away now. I didn't listen to it. I pushed hard, the cuts of the key clearing the rust and detritus from a dead-bolt that hadn't been touched for years, and the door finally opened. The creaking of the hinges was straight out of a horror movie. For the first time in years, a blade of sunlight sliced through the room.

From the doorway, all I could see was the mess. The floor was strewn with books, papers, pans, shards of broken crockery. A table had been upturned and thrown against a wall, alongside two plastic chairs. A shelf had come off the wall, shattering glasses and casserole tops. There were mouse droppings everywhere, like a layer of dust. It was impossible to tell where the work of the Carabinieri ended, and the decay of abandonment began.

I had come equipped with a flashlight. Without moving from where I was, I shone the beam around the room. I saw a kitchen worktop, with a sink, a stove, and a gas canister. A worn-out two-seater with its foam innards spewing from the slits that had been cut during the search. On the left, a dresser, its doors yanked off, and two empty drawers left on top. Apart from the books, there were hardly any other items. An electric heater and a table fan. An opening with no door, to the side of the kitchenette, led to the other room. That was as much as I could see.

Looking for proof that you're not involved can be danger-ous; you risk finding it. I hadn't taken one step yet, but it was clear from the very start. There was no sign of us there. Of me. What I was surveying was the den of a stranger. The style and taste of the furnishings, the way my father had decorated the dump, recalled nothing of the man I had always known. Cheap materials: tin and chipboard. This might have given me comfort: the place was makeshift, a temporary abode, not somewhere you leave your signature embellishments. And yet, there was a dining table, a kitchenette, a bedroom. The bare necessities. For staying there a few days, perhaps, far away from everything. A break from the same old life. An oasis of peace, a few feet away from a little girl in an iron cage. The myriad of seminars, work trips, conferences, lecture circuits, awards—even when Mom was still around—flashed before my eyes. He would come back looking exhausted, too tired to report much about all the boring dinners he was constantly being invited to. He would always call at precisely the same time to say everything was going well. I suddenly pictured him calling from the gas station at the end of the dirt track. And then driving back to his secret den and warming up some soup in silence.

As I threw open the shutters, fat spiders dropped from the jambs. Only then did I notice that the damp had penetrated so deeply that the walls were mapped with stains.

The bedroom was half the size of the living space. The single mattress had been tossed off the sprung bed base, which in its turn had been turned, legs up. The dimensions of his existence there hurt me: a life for one, away from the family. The bedside table had also been gutted, as had the two-door wardrobe, which was empty. A lamp with a plastic shade had been thrown into a corner, where it had gathered a crust of dirt. In the opposite corner, there was a heap of damp blankets and clothes, no doubt riddled with nesting animals. Poking out of the pile was a red, polo-necked sweater I'd never seen my father wear, and a pair of plastic slip-on shoes that were nothing like the velvet slippers he would put on as soon as he walked into the house.

And then there was the bathroom. It was little bigger than a cubbyhole; just a toilet and a washbasin. The floor curved down to a drain in the middle. To shower, you simply flooded the place. I tried turning the faucet. The response was a hollow rumble of pipes and vents.

After clearing the land, I started on the house. The recycling depot saw me arrive with doors and furniture chopped to pieces. Taking the ax to everything gave me satisfaction. It was good to wreck the wardrobe with hammer blows to its side. I didn't salvage anything. I enjoyed scrubbing the walls, scraping off layers of filth. I chose a bright white paint for the walls, inside and out, replacing that lifeless yellow he had covered everything in, who knows when. I put in a baseboard, restored the window jambs, and sanded the shutters to their original wooden surface. I then varnished them to look like cherrywood, the same color as the fence. The plumber who came to replace the water pipes and toilet brought along a surly young assistant, who acted as if he were his bodyguard. The team of Albanians I paid to put in the new kitchen took no notice; nor did the boy who came to get the boat as soon as he'd read the ad. My terms were clear: anybody willing to haul the boat away could have it, as long as they took care of the papers. He didn't care one bit that a string of murdered girls had been transported in it. All he cared about was the money he thought he could make restoring the cabin cruiser. He took the trailer, too.

It was becoming all too clear: eventually, I would have to tackle the container.

Against all odds, the first night I slept in the restored property passed without mishap. I slept soundly, uninterrupted. I may have been playing for time, but I decided that before opening the iron mouth, I would paint it a nice bright color. From its original cattle-truck brown (so well camouflaged you couldn't see it from the road if you didn't know it was there), I transformed it into a vivid red. It took two coats, which I applied carefully, without scrimping. It was like signing a declaration. External appearances say a great deal about what is inside. Perhaps everything.

People in the town hardly saw me anymore. Just the odd

foray to grab my mail and the few things I needed: clothes, my laptop, tools, and material for my miniatures. They watched me leave, laden with boxes. My dear neighbors, mirrors of civilized society, were stuck there. They hadn't had the same luck as me: a flush bank account that would allow them to change everything about their lives, from one day to the next. I wonder whether my father had planned all this: leaving me an inheritance so that I could get on with my life after he was jailed.

Finally, I knew the time had come.

Forcing the container open was no walk in the park; the latches and bolts had rusted after years of disuse, and I struggled to pull them free. There was no catharsis involved; just sweat and fatigue. Cursing under my breath. Until there was a clanging of iron. The door on the right was stuck, as if it had been soldered shut. Another battle. Hanging onto the vertical bars, I yanked as hard as I could, hoping the whole thing wouldn't come off in my face. The door opened a chink. A hairline crack into the void, just big enough to slide something in to use as leverage.

Prying the container open made the most horrific noise; a wild roar and a scream of agony combined. A whiff of heat enveloped me, like the breath of a sleeping dragon.

It's always the same: when you actually meet the monster of your nightmares, it's almost disappointing. A giant cage with nothing in it, picked clean to the bone by the Carabinieri. During the trial, Martini had told me that Laura's prison hadn't been particularly horrifying. There had been no meat hooks, knives, or other atrocities. Admittedly, Laura had been held in chains, but they were long enough to allow her to get out of bed, either to answer her calls of nature (two hermetically sealed jars), to get a drink, or to fetch a cookie. On the right-hand side of the container, the steel shelving unit used to store food was still there. Opposite was a desk—my father had provided books, notebooks, and pencils—with a table lamp on it. The cord had been pulled through a hole drilled in the wall, and plugged into a socket in the house. I could see the perfect little white circle in the dark, like a bullet hole. Laura had not been driven crazy by long periods of darkness in between the periodic visits from her jailer. If a storm tripped the fuse, though, days and days might have gone by before the light came back. The investigators had gained access to the electricity bills. A little girl, who then became an adolescent and later a young woman, was the one who had consumed most of it. Once a week, she would receive new batteries for her Walkman. There was a whole collection of cassette tapes of popular hits of the day, alongside a complete set of children's story tapes that used to be sold with a weekly magazine at the newsagents. Another thing that Martini reported about the trial sent a cold shiver down my spine, "The victim declared that in fourteen years of imprisonment, your father never spoke a word to her."

One Sunday, we went out for a drive with no particular destination in mind. I'd just gotten my learner's permit, and I was thrilled. I couldn't wait to show him what I'd learned in my driving lessons. Owning a brand-new car, and not being allowed to drive it, was agony. In any case, I wanted to admire myself as I enacted the gesture of opening the door on the driver's side and saying, "I'm driving," while my father, for the first time, opened the passenger door. It was the beginning of an important new chapter.

He was unconcerned. He allowed himself to be driven and kept his eyes on the road. He didn't make a single comment. Not even when I took my foot off the clutch too early at the traffic light in Via Salceta. The car stalled in the middle of the crossroads, and all the other drivers were honking furiously at us. He waited for my panic to run its course. I was already imagining the ignominy of having to open the door, climb out, and switch places with my dad in front of everyone. And then curling up in the passenger seat wanting to disappear, my face hot with shame, while an adult took the wheel instead of a novice who had created a traffic jam for no reason. But he just sat there, staring ahead of him. He had a placid smile on his face, completely indifferent to the savages who were honking their horns around us, despite the red L decal on the front and back license plates. The worst of them was a small woman in a Fiat Panda with a nervous little dog yapping at the windscreen. My father only opened his mouth when, after one or two failed attempts to start the car, I finally got my nerve back as the lights were about to turn yellow.

"I'm hungry," he said. "Take me somewhere."

There must have been some mysterious current in the air; somehow, we ended up at a shack where they used to serve food just off the provincial road. It was only a few miles from the dirt track. Nobody told me to go in that direction, but as soon as we were out of town, I drove onto the four-lane national highway and headed straight for that place as if I had been called there. It was filled with truckers, and we sat outside on a bench under a pergola that looked out onto fields. It was a lovely sunny day. I felt like I was in a film. We were only about 20 miles from home, but the fact that I had driven that distance myself made me feel like the master of the universe. We didn't talk about anything special. My father was good at giving just the right weight to silences; he knew how to gift wrap them to make them feel precious. We sat there enjoying that new dimension.

Toward the end of the meal, he said, "What's that there?"

I looked at my shoulder. A twig must have fallen onto it. I tried to flick it off, but it was stuck to my T-shirt. I tried again and saw that it was moving.

A stick insect. I'd never seen one close up. If it had been a spider, I would have leaped out of my seat, but this creature was different. I didn't find it nearly as revolting as a locust or a mantis. I was pleased not to be disgusted by it. I sat still, looking completely unflustered. Actually, I was so confident that I grabbed my paper napkin, picked the insect up, and put it on the table as if it were the most normal thing in the world.

It looked like a creature from outer space. Like some of the monsters in Matteo Lorenzi's glass cases. It was completely immobile. My first thought was, "How can it live?" It was truly identical to a twig; impossible to tell the difference. I wondered how many stick insects I had trodden on in my life without even realizing; how many had been caught in my hair . . . and asked myself what purpose they could possibly serve. It was one of those encounters that made you interrogate nature's design: for some reason or other, there were strange beings living on this earth. They may have populated it long before mankind poked its nose out of the primordial gruel. I gazed at it for a few minutes. I was about to blow it away when a dome of glass was lowered onto it.

My father had used the bowl the shack had provided as an ashtray. The stick insect was now trapped inside.

"We could keep it," I heard a voice say.

I looked at my father.

"What would we do with it?"

I had never expressed a desire to have a terrarium at home. He shrugged.

"Just to have it. Let's see what it does."

What was it supposed to do? It was motionless. After a while, though, we watched it shed its mask. Its antennae started moving as if testing the new environment. To hell with camouflage; its life was at risk, so it had to busy itself with survival. There was no way anyone could empathize with it; it didn't have the languid eyes of a puppy. My father's unusually gratuitous gesture—he would always observe things from a distance, without interacting or grandstanding—had triggered something, however. I picked up the ashtray and put it back the right way up on the table. Using the paper napkin, I freed our strange guest, dropping it into a nearby flower pot. My father smiled.

"You're so sensitive," he said.

I have transformed the shipping container into a workshop for my miniatures. Matteo Lorenzi would be proud. The desk is my worktop, and the steel shelf unit is a display case for my most successful models. Laura's army is almost complete, a tightly-packed battalion representing her new life: Laura in a black down jacket and a yellow scarf waiting for the subway; Laura in a crowd wearing a denim skirt and flip-flops; Laura miles away, the gaping black holes dragging her into another place. I'm modeling her here, in the very place where she had been held prisoner.

If I told Naima, she would probably have me committed. She wouldn't get it. She keeps talking to me about socialization. She would like to hear about walks on the seafront, evenings at the disco, confirmation that I was unabashedly embracing the world again. I invent one-night stands and make up stories about my evening entertainment. I dish them out so naturally that for a moment I fall for them myself. I create false memories that are tailor-made to fulfill her expectations. I tell her about young women, with a taste for the macabre, who come and sit on the bar stool next to me and ask for a drink. I tell her about older women, in their mid-forties, who know my history: the son of that guy, but he's got a bulging bank account. Gossip travels fast in a small town. I tell my therapist things that are so absurd they don't need any explanation, and are thus considered true.

What I do not tell her is that I am invested in Laura; in her saving herself. I feel there's no time to waste. At the same time, I realize maybe that's exactly what she needs: to waste a little time, of her own volition. To sit in her room doing nothing, music playing in the background. Like in the container. Except she'd be the one deciding, this time. To be able to put her shoes on and go out. Or to throw herself off a fourth-floor balcony. That would also be her choice. Freedom can open up a surprising range of options.

During the trial, the prosecution claimed that one of the reasons my father chose little girls was because they would be incapable of committing suicide. Or, let's say, in the weird game he was playing, he was relying on that card. When Martini reported this detail, the ashen eyes of the stick insect came back to my mind: "Let's see what it does." That phrase sums up his perversion. I feel as though I'm the one under the glass. By getting himself caught, he has enclosed me in a bell jar. Had he calculated this, too? Am I his final experiment?

Milan is immense. Looking for a parking space drives me crazy; everything drives me crazy. People don't notice me; invisibility is my daily bread. I seek anonymity but, on those streets, it borders on the inhuman. Laura is a shard of light in a toxic city of busy people. In her eyes, everything is a novelty. She is amazed by the giant billboards, by the size of the buildings. Having gotten out of a dark tunnel after fourteen years, she hasn't locked herself into another cage. Into a family. Or her mind. It would have been entirely natural; a safe haven, where the deprivations of captivity she had suffered for more than half her lifetime might be forgotten. Re-training herself to live can't be easy. But Laura is tough. And Francesca is a good therapist.

Owing to my pressing work schedule, we opted for monthly sessions. Her office felt like home. The first time I set foot inside I absorbed everything: the paintings, the objects, the smell. In her eyes, I must have looked like a nervous control freak. That played in my favor, at least. I listed my symptoms: anxiety, insomnia, sudden episodes where I'm overtaken by a sense of unreality, a feeling I'm fading away. They were all real enough. Working at managerial level in pharmaceuticals requires taking on a great deal of responsibility, and can be incredibly stressful. I was always traveling. I would sometimes wake up with a start with no idea where I was. For a few seconds, I would lie there, conscious but empty, as if my mind had been rebooted. It was an effort to remember what my name was (and I wasn't lying about that, either). The sensation stayed with me all day, long after I had returned to myself. I would munch Xanax with my breakfast coffee and biscuits. No family. Not even a girlfriend, just occasional fleeting encounters. Switching my phone off during the session was a struggle; it cut me off completely. She saw me as the archetype of a workaholic. There were many people who aspired to be like me.

The plan was to check out that area of Laura's life, and then vanish into thin air. One session; at most, two. But then I got a taste for it. Francesca mustn't know it, but discussing the psychological disorders of another me creates a kind of suspension, a truce from myself. I never prepare for the sessions; I just let the other guy's life surprise me while I sit there in the therapy chair. "How are we doing today?" she asks, and I start talking. I invent new episodes, plumbing the depths of my childhood. By the end of the session, when I get out onto the street, I am cleansed. While Naima takes care of the real me, Francesca is dealing with a projection that reverberates within me—who knows where or why—to the point that I often find myself walking a fair distance after our sessions with a smile on my lips. In addition, she provides reassurance. Laura is in good hands.

I can see she's doing well from Facebook. Her profile picture is a photo taken from above of her dirty, white Converse sneakers, splashing in a muddy puddle (there's a barely-visible shadow in the reflection of the water). In the top right-hand corner, there's a stubbed-out cigarette, and in the left, a leaf reduced almost to mulch. Laura takes photos like this. Details. A recurrent theme is the sky; a spectrum from blinding blue to a metallic purple-gray that looks like it's smashing into the buildings. There is an abundance of sunsets. (Online cynics would yawn, as they make every effort to distance themselves from sentimentality. But what do they know? There are millions of ghastly people out there, ready to dish out an opinion on everything. They don't give a damn about the symbols that govern a life. They love using ellipses.) She also likes crowd scenes. Pictures taken quickly, often out of focus, with blurred outlines and indistinguishable faces; people hurrying from one place to another and little else. The useless corner of a street. The neon sign of a coin-operated laundromat, somebody waiting inside. The aluminum-foil container of fried chicken from a Chinese takeaway opened on someone's knees on a park bench. Five years have gone by, but she is still in awe of the outside world. Laura has two hundred and sixty-four friends.

I am one of them, with the *nom de guerre* Ulto Bear, hero of the D.A. (Deliverance Army). My profile image is taken from *Total Invasion 4*, which is shared by thousands of kids all over the world. I like giving free publicity to my friend who is a huge success in California. (I'm also happy to discover that Matteo Lorenzi has a beautiful wife and a daughter named Jade.)

Building a realistic profile of a nerd takes a long time. Months of sharing, posting, liking, and reposting. Ulto Bear's main interests are videogames, illustrations, graphic novels, and the latest TV series. Plus, the world of miniatures. I share teasers and join in on all the forums. It's a gargantuan effort keeping up with the crazed herd of contributors, who always have a comeback ready. Adjusting my banter to appear ironic is a titanic task in itself; achieving cynicism almost kills me, but I occasionally succeed. I create a circle of friends in no time at all. Kids write to me personally, complimenting me on my miniatures or, more often than not, patting me on the back for my efforts and gushing with advice. I accept their tips gracefully and thank them. It's amazing to see the number of "likes" I can collect when I share images of the pirates and little monsters that I used to make twenty years ago. My more recent miniatures are less popular by far. I ransack my old school friend's page. Since he sells mostly to kids, he's everywhere on social media and always well-informed about the latest updates. Some of his scoops are enough to make aficionados drool; maybe he gets paid for that too. He's a real star, with more than 300,000 followers. I grab material wherever I can find it and post it. My only rule is never to post anything personal. It's always a temptation to go off on an emotional joyride, but I hold back. At most, I'll open a Word document and vent my feelings there.

After all this effort, I felt my identity was relatively well established. My first friend request was to a science fiction freak on Laura's contact list. His obsession, which had become his mission in life, was to rewrite the final episode of *Lost*. He had been so disappointed by the finale, and had such a high opinion of his own talent, that he was convinced he had the tools to dot a few i's and cross a few t's. Francesco Garrin (alias Altair76). He wrote in block capitals, attracting the attention of the outspoken. He cursed a lot, as part of his subversive act. There were times when I wanted to reach out and hug him. He updated his popular blog once a week, keeping his followers on tenterhooks with continuous announcements that his masterpiece was about to come out, and that he may have found a publisher daring enough to take it on. I played along for a while. I graced his bullshit with multiple exclamation points, without believing a thing. At the same time, I worked at making my posts go viral. Ulto Bear interacted with that particular page, often triggering a flurry of messages back and forth. Some went badly. A small-town twenty-year-old told me to fuck off before we made peace on Messenger. Another new contact. I was getting closer.

I had to stay cool and not hurry things. I hung out with the misunderstood genius for a while; after a lot of arguing and exchanging views, I acquired a few more scalps. I remained under the radar for a few weeks: just my miniatures (I was surprisingly good by then), waiting for the new season of *Game of Thrones* with bated breath, and ploughing through literally thousands of words devoted to the rumors about the release of a film based on *Breaking Bad*—were they credible or was it fake news?

Then I did it: "Add Friend." We had quite a few mutual contacts by that point.

Days went by, and Laura still hadn't accepted me. My phone was stuck to my hand; I refreshed my page every ten seconds. She continued to go onto Facebook, post photos of clouds, windows, streaks of sunlight on cement (her profile was public, which made me wonder if she even knew what that meant?). One morning, I woke up and found the notification I had been waiting for: my friend request had been accepted that night. I waited until the afternoon to write to her. The main thing to avoid was looking like the person I actually was—a peeping Tom—so she wouldn't block me in the space of a week. My palms sweating, I typed a private message: "Hi. Thanks for your friendship." Followed by a smiley face.

I sometimes wonder whether someone is keeping an eye on me. All things considered, there may well be an expert hacker, who has decided to get his life back into shape and has started working for the Carabinieri. Cross-checking all the data, anyone could reconstruct my interactions on the web. It's a risk I'm willing to take. If I were ever exposed, I would tell them, heart in hand, that I'm not doing anything wrong. Playing the guardian angel to the girl my father imprisoned for fourteen years keeps me alive. I feel responsible; all this time with a guilty conscience that won't go away. They can ask my therapist. I mean Naima, of course, not Francesca. My Milan therapist is another matter. I'm obsessed by the idea that Laura deserves a good life. The steel shelf unit in the container is proof enough. I spend most of my days, curved over my worktop, in that very container. A kind of expiation. A kind of madness. I'm being held captive in a glass jar: to begin with, I'm motionless, trying not to get disoriented. Then I start to move my antennae.

Laura has never answered my message, but she hasn't unfriended me, either. The only time I react directly is when she posts photographs of her shadow. I can't resist a *Like*. Every click almost gives me a heart attack.

Her profile reveals nothing about her; not even what her hands look like. It's impossible to know what she looks like, what color the walls of her bedroom are. If you don't know her, the only thing you can see are deformed silhouettes: long legs, faded profiles, blurred reflections. Maybe that's how she sees herself. Day by day, she is putting herself into greater focus, and I am encouraging her.

She never writes anything, or posts comments. Only photos and songs. I swoop down onto these like a demon, fleshing out my one and only playlist with the unequivocal name "Laura." Her music is the background of my daily life.

In general, however, I'm concerned. Being on social media so anonymously reveals a great deal. She has never posted a photo of the boyfriend she's been seeing for a few months (his profile is private). I suppose they may have talked about it, but if I were him, I would feel excluded. Not significant enough to be exhibited to the digital world. The actual physical relationship, the talking and eye contact, is what counts, of course. And yet, for a while now, another form of communication has existed, one where everyone is exposed, for better or for worse. Not displaying someone in the digital dimension of your life is a way to bar them from a piece of you, even when that someone is a person with whom you go out to dinner, or whatever. I wonder what she's told him about who she is and where she comes from.

Please, please, please let me get what I want . . . after listening to the song a hundred times, it has become a mantra. The words have become meaningless and the music explodes in a vibration that speaks like the wind. Just like the wind that is blowing now, making the doors of the container creak. A storm is brewing. The willow branches are whipping against the iron walls. I'm focused on the little steel wire approximation in my hands. I bulk out the curve of the hip. I stare at the photo under the lamplight. I took it furtively last time I was following her: Laura, distracted, her thoughts miles away, in a subway carriage. On the Yellow Line. Everyone's indifference is a safe haven for her. When she obliterates herself like that, she often misses her stop. She doesn't seem to mind; rather, she smiles to herself. She lets another stop go by.

There is a loud bang and the lamp flickers. The container is being buffeted by gusts of wind. The clang that follows chills my blood as I understand what has happened: the vertical bar has dropped. Locking me in.

During the initial search of the house I received an arrest warrant, too. Protective custody, they called it. Living there, I might contaminate the evidence.

"What evidence?" I asked.

Nobody bothered to answer.

Martini came to the precinct at Via Saffi the next morning and accompanied me into the interview room.

"Luca, we need to talk."

I almost laughed in his face.

"At the very least."

They had arrested my father in his pajama bottoms, his mouth full of onion frittata. They hadn't even given him time to clean himself up. His glasses were still on the table, and he couldn't read a word without them. I had spent the night in jail, too, and I still didn't know what we were being accused of. Martini was the one to tell me.

I had to listen to a long story about a ragtag band of backwater thugs: three ex-cons who had graduated from burglaries to raiding pharmacies, but had never upped the ante and attempted a bank robbery. They were no geniuses: mean-faced, armed with knives, they were of the "give me the cash and ciao" school of robbery. No trouble; just a few fights here and there. Or dramatic escapes. Martini told me that the day before, a sprightly old man, hardened by the evening news, had heard a suspicious noise and grabbed his hunting rifle. This had been outside a villa in the San Luigi residential area that attracted waves of local crooks. The police had been called immediately, and the goons had been pinpointed on the four-lane national highway heading out of town. There had been a chase.

I stared at the family attorney with the expression of someone falling from a sixth-floor window: what did I or my father have to do with these people? He looked down at the desk and cleared his throat twice.

"This is the hard part," he said.

Following his story, I pictured the stolen car roaring along the road at over 100 miles per hour, the flashing blue lights of the Carabinieri who were hot on their heels, like wolves. The hoodlums eventually realize that if they stay on the main road they'll soon be in handcuffs. Taking the first exit possible, they lead their tail onto the provincial road, and then into a tangle of minor roads. Still exposed, their only chance is to find cover in the woods. They make a U-turn onto a dirt track and almost end up in a ditch. (Martini sighs. "If that had happened, we wouldn't be here now.")

The patrol car loses pace and has to slow down, because of the cloud of dust in front of it. The thugs turn their headlights off, leaving the Carabinieri's lights to collide with a dense wall of fog. Which, at a certain point, lifts and they accelerate, almost crashing into the criminals' car, abandoned with its doors open on the edge of a beech wood. Right in front of a little property. ("For the record: they didn't catch the lowlives, who disappeared into the woods. But they did find something else.")

In an iron cell, mobile phones are as good as dead. Moreover, I'm not as canny as the man who jailed Laura. I've looked for her for so long that I've finally found her. In fact, I've become her. The small detail that unites us is that nobody knows I'm here, inside my father's stomach.

I have no tools; I have nothing. I am deep inside the eyes of an eight-year-old girl. Short of breath, monsters in every corner. My voice bounces off the iron walls with a metallic echo. The lamp gives me light: the source of life. A sudden thirst. Everything is sudden. Six paces one way; six the other. The sum total of the container. After an hour, only the essentials count: food and water. Above all, water. Then I hear a crash— the storm has tripped the fuse. The darkness cuts through me like a blade of ice, taking my breath away.

THE BOX

Laura knows she's old enough to be alone in the living room, but she's still scared. Every morning, she wonders what it is that makes her nervous, but she can't explain it. She's scared; that's all. The room changes, even during the day. There are noises that weren't there before. Once in a film she heard someone say, "Summon ghosts and they'll come." If you think about them, they prick up their ears. So, you walk differently, with the idea that someone is behind you. You turn and see nobody. An invisible hand brushes against your hair. You can tell yourself over and over that it's just a gust of wind, but it's no use.

She has her own way of staving those feelings off: singing. She starts by humming softly, with no words: "M-mmm . . . M-mmm . . . " It keeps her company. In the meantime, she colors in her vacation homework book. She keeps her eyes on the pictures and lets her hair fall on both sides to blinker her, so that she can only see the page. Mamma has already gone upstairs to do the work she does in her bedroom. They need to make ends meet. She says this to her husband a lot: "Make ends meet." Every time she goes to her room to work, there are angry faces, glares, and unexpressed protests. The little girl is here and the parents must control themselves. Anyway, there's no need to say anything. Anyone can see that when they talk about bills or due dates, all they want to do is say mean things to each other. One passes the mayonnaise to the other, and it's like they're throwing knives instead of doing a favor. At dinner, the veins in their necks are as thick as phone cables. As they shovel down their food, they swallow the poison they can't spit out onto the table, not with Laura there. That's what gives them heartburn. Especially her father. One time out of three, when he's finished the meal, he'll open the medicine drawer, pull out a bottle, and send a pill down with the dregs of his wine.

Laura knows her mother does a special job and that she's not allowed to talk to anyone about it. Not even Martina Cancelli, even though she is her best friend, and they once swore they were like sisters. Sometimes she thinks: even if I wanted to, what would I tell her? "My mother locks herself in her room all morning and chats on the phone." She has no idea what she talks about, or who she's talking to. All Laura knows is she has to stay in the living room. At the coffee table with her schoolbooks, and the TV turned up high. She's allowed to answer the door to the mailman, but if he needs a signature, she's not to let him in. She's to go upstairs and knock on the door, without touching the handle. Her mother rushes down. She has to hurry, like when Nonna's on the phone, and she says, "Ma, there's a pan on the burner . . . " and hangs up immediately. She sometimes says it even when there's nothing on the stove. She's always in her tracksuit when she runs down the stairs to sign for a package.

She stops at midday. Instead of getting some fresh air, she shuts herself into another room; this time, the bathroom. She puts music on loud, but she doesn't sing. Laura may be wrong, but it sounds like her mother is talking to herself in there. She sounds angry with someone, and every now and again lets out a shout that she can't seem to control.

When her mother comes into the living room, Laura's not scared anymore. When, a few minutes later, she thinks back to how scared she was, she realizes how stupid she was being. She can't understand what she was peeing her pants for. At least she's not behind in her vacation homework, but she still has some to do. It's not the middle of August yet, but September will be here in no time. When school starts, she'll hand in the completed workbook to her teacher, Mrs. Pina, and she'll get the first gold star of the year. It's not that satisfying, though, because she gives everyone gold stars—even the boys who leave the last pages blank. Her teacher doesn't even notice, or she pretends not to. She takes a quick look, sticks a gold star in, and goes on to the next one. There are some kids who are so lazy they only do half the book and they still get the same as the kids at the top of the class. Take Elia Favilli, for example. Once Laura told her father about him. He answered, looking at her mother pointedly: "Those who do, do; those who don't, sooner or later will be found out."

There are some mornings when time stands still, and Laura is so scared, she can only half breathe. The weight on her chest is unbearable, especially when it rains. Especially when she looks through the window and sees Martina Cancelli hanging out on her own in the park opposite, looking bored. When Laura sees her best friend, she waves to her, and Martina waves back. They smile at one another. Sometimes, Martina calls up to her: "Come down, just for a minute!" Laura is sorry she has to say no. There's always a battle. Her friend insists, and she opens her arms wide: she has to stay inside, her mother doesn't want her to go out; she prefers to keep an eye on her. Martina scowls and goes and sits on the swing with her head down, scratching at the sand with the toes of her sandals for a few minutes. Laura looks behind her, as if a shadow has actually crossed the corridor, flitted through the door, and gone down into the basement. Her heart is pounding. There are times when she gives in. She checks the time—eleven something. The TV is blaring. Whether she stays home or flies to the moon, it wouldn't make any difference. So, she makes up her mind, goes to the front door, and opens it.

The morning light is glorious. On the doorstep, the sun shines on her face, so hot it feels like she's cooking. Martina Cancelli jumps up and starts towards her, but Laura puts her hand out to stop her. The gesture means, "Stay there. Mamma doesn't want a mess in the house while she's working to make ends meet." Her friend takes no notice and comes closer. Laura is forced to make a decision: if she doesn't want her nosy friend to snoop around, she'd better go herself. They meet at the fence; one inside the park, the other outside. Martina Cancelli can't understand what has changed since the beginning of June. Laura used to come out to play in the park without making such a fuss.

"Are you coming?" she asks.

Laura speaks so softly it sounds like her voice is under her feet.

"I can't."

Martina Cancelli looks at the house.

"Why not?"

Laura looks up at her parents' bedroom window.

"Because I can't."

"Shall we make some mud cakes?"

Martina Cancelli has no idea how her friend's tummy twists and turns when she hears this.

"I need to finish my vacation homework."

"Can I come to your house? Let's pretend we're getting married . . . "

"Later."

"When?"

Always the same questions.

"Later."

Martina Cancelli looks down again.

"Later, I'm going to the beach," she says. She has her own problems, too. There's a man called Ignazio who works as a barman at the Orchid Beach Club, and her mother has been taking three-hour coffee breaks with him lately. Laura gazes at her friend's suntan and feels sad. She lives by the sea, and she's stuck indoors in her living room all day. It's getting harder and harder to bear. Martina Cancelli studies her face.

"Did they tell you not to speak to me anymore?"

Martina is mean. She's making things worse for her, as usual. Martina thinks Laura's the mean one. Laura feels as though she's about to burst into tears. She remembers once standing on the doorstep talking to Martina, as quiet as a mouse, when the draught slammed the door shut behind her. She had to walk around the house and go in through the garage. The idea of having to do that now on her own makes her want to die.

"You know," she says, "that my mother does a special job."

"Talking to aliens?"

Laura sighs. Maybe it's true.

"I don't know," she answers.

"Come on, just two minutes!" Martina pleads.

It's hard to say no to your best friend all the time, especially when you've sworn that she's like the sister you thought, until recently, you were going to have, but who never came along. All because of the ends, apparently, that they suddenly can't make meet.

The 167 West neighborhood is quite isolated; there is no way of telling you are ten minutes from the sea. Many of the duplexes are rented out for the summer, but during the day the place is deserted. Everyone goes to the beach. There are some who get up at 5 A.M. to occupy the front row with their beach umbrellas, and then go home for breakfast. The funniest thing is some of the families from the neighborhood. They live with boxes stashed on top of their wardrobes and clogging up their hallways from September to June, then as soon as the season opens, they take everything away leaving only the bare necessities. They strip the house of photos of weddings and birthdays and move in with their parents-in-law in another part of the town for the whole summer. Packed like sardines in the heat, tormented by mosquitoes, it is a sacrifice they are loath to make, but at least by the end of September they have four months' rent in their pockets. Others use the time to travel. Once Laura asked her mother, "Why don't we go away like the Parisi family?" Her mother glared at her. She was staring at the water bill, as if the time and date of her death were written on it. She didn't bother to answer. When she asked her father, however, he was quite clear. "I break my back every day so that, when I come home, I can feel as though at least a corner of the house belongs to me and not the bank." For him, staying at number 35 on Via Bassi is a point of honor.

The mornings when Laura is unable to say no to her best friend are adventures, even though nothing special ever happens. The feeling that she might be found out alters the quality of time, leading her from the anguish of home to life on the other side of the gate, even though there are only cats dozing in the shade of the box hedges there. The two friends go deeper into the park, under the thicker canopies. They usually play on the roundabout they have ridden on since they were toddlers, which is in a more hidden corner of the park, and tell each other their secrets. In the end, they get bored anyway because, after a while, there's not much to do on the spinning wheel, except listen to cicadas and the very occasional car that passes by. But at least they are getting bored together. Laura keeps an eye on the time. Her gaze drifts over the park and focuses on her front door; she's ready to run for it if the mailman, or some other trouble, presents itself. She must be on the sofa when her mother comes down in her bathrobe, with a towel wrapped around her head, and heads straight for the kitchen, where she lights up a cigarette. She smokes leaning on the sink, her jaw slack, her expression vacant. Then she calls Laura to help get lunch ready. Sometimes her mother notices something about her. "What's that smirk on your face?" she might say, smiling a little to herself. For a moment, she is the mamma Laura has always known. But it doesn't last long.

When it's time to go, Martina Cancelli starts throwing a fit. It's always the same: Laura has to go and Martina doesn't want to be left on her own. They make pact after pact: two more minutes, forty seconds more, twenty . . . Or they have a fight. Martina Cancelli, feeling abandoned, folds her arms and sulks. She doesn't understand it's not Laura's fault. She doesn't want to understand. The idea of being left alone and then spending an endless afternoon at the Orchid Beach Club, upsets her. She has one of her temper tantrums.

"All you think about is yourself. Nice sister you are."

Laura's face burns. Martina's the selfish one. They go on like this for a bit, while the big hand on her watch keeps ticking. There comes a point when Laura really can't wait any longer, whether they're arguing or not. She jumps off the wheel. Her best friend hates the idea of Laura being the first to take off, and so she runs away without looking back, as if to say, "You're not the one leaving, *I am*." She abandons Laura, who is torn between her desire to make peace and her fear of being caught. She doesn't call out to her. She gives vent to her frustration by stamping her foot and muttering under her breath, "What an idiot." Then she crosses the park on her own, carefully choosing the path under the trees. Where there is shade. And nobody can see her.

The doctor man doesn't speak. Laura tries to pull herself up but he puts a hand on her chest as if to say, "Stay still. You need to rest." He examines the little girl from head to toe; he can see what he needs to see immediately. Laura's so tired she feels as heavy as a rock. To lift an arm, she needs to concentrate all her attention on where her arm should be, but not much seems to happen. Everything around her is hazy; she looks around, and the walls vanish into mist. She has a bitter taste in her mouth. She can feel it in her nose, like a strange tickle. Her face is burning, prickling all over.

Like that time with the black-cherry ice cream. One minute, she was with her mother at the market stand, the next, there was a man with a beard above her, repeating, "Hey little doll, can you hear me?" That was when the whole boring anemia thing started: iron supplements and horsemeat steaks that turned her stomach just looking at them. Her father making snide comments about how much they cost, which would make Laura feel sick twice over.

This doctor man doesn't say a thing. He appears and disappears from behind the veils Laura feels she has on both sides of her eyes. He plumps up her pillow. He touches a contraption that has been hung around her neck. The little girl would like to ask, "Where's Mamma?" but the sounds that come out of her mouth are garbled, even to her. They echo in her head like the stupid songs she sings to scare off the ghosts.

The bad part isn't shaking off the sleepiness that is pinning her to the bed. The bad part is that Laura has been found out. She tries to think, but she can't remember crossing either the park or the road, nor can she remember closing the gate. She must have fainted before that, maybe frightening some of the old ladies on the sidewalk. And her mother, too. She would have had to interrupt her phone calls. Even though she wasn't making ends meet.

It was all because of her stupid best friend. Martina had gone away, leaving her with a brick in the place of her stomach. Mouthfuls of poison, like her father when he finishes his dinner, his eyes on his plate. With the anemia, the anger, the ghosts, and the bills that put everyone in a bad mood, she

sometimes has a funny turn. "It could be to do with her emotions, too," the doctor with the beard had said that time when
she had already been sitting up, sucking on the candy she had
been given.

This doctor man is drenched in sweat. He leans over the little girl, fiddling, fixing, streams of sweat running down his
nose and dripping onto her face. One lands on her lips; it's
salty. Laura doesn't want to, but she can't help it: she swallows
it, setting in motion a series of cogs she didn't even know
existed. A tiny drop of saliva scratches in her throat, like she'd
swallowed gravel.

She finally understands: she's thirsty but doesn't know how
to tell him. The doctor man should be able to see it. But he
isn't that good. He's tightening a tourniquet. It doesn't hurt,
but Laura feels her skin doesn't belong to her. She looks away;
seeing the needles for the IV drip or the blood test makes her
heart beats faster. All she wants to do is go back home, meet
Martina Cancelli on her side of the fence, and tell her that
being best friends is something else altogether. And break her
oath to be sisters, even though she would be on her own again.
It's all the same, in the end.

He doesn't look at her, so Laura doesn't look at him. She
lies beside the iron wall without touching it, because it's boil-
ing hot. She only turns around when the man goes out, taking
the garbage with him. Laura sees the light coming from the
door at the end of the big room. At first, all she can see is a
white rectangle, with an outline of a man getting smaller and
smaller until it disappears. Then her eyes gradually get used to
the place and start picking out details. A fragment of the
house: a gutter, for example. Or a few trees, a stretch of garden, a few feet of fencing. Beyond, nothing. Not one building,
not a curve of a hill. Just fields. Sky. A few birds on their way
somewhere else. The sound of water swishing in buckets. A

cough. When he comes back, the little girl turns around and faces the other way again.

Going crazy, pulling her hair out, yelling, kicking the iron wall was no use. She tried everything. Once, she was so angry she emptied out the toilet buckets. He looked on as the mess mingled on the floor. He looked blank for a moment, like a retard. Then he walked out, taking no notice of her screaming, locked the door, and left her there. A minute later, she heard the car engine revving. The tires, as always, screeching on the gravel.

Doing nothing is his method for teaching Laura the rules. He lets her stew in her own juices. If she breaks something, she won't have it anymore. If she throws her food on the floor, he doesn't pick it up. Maggots grow, and the stench rises in the heat. Like with her piss and shit. He left her there for two days. Covering the floor with tissues was not enough; Laura had to step in the revolting stuff to get to the buckets.

When he comes, the first thing he does is bring in a tub of water, a sponge, some soap, a change of clothes, and a tooth-brush. He puts everything on the floor, at the end of the bed, and then he goes out. Laura needs to use the minutes at her disposal wisely, without dawdling. Her skin is even thirstier than she is. The foam stirs her from her lethargy, from the hours and hours of neglect. She rushes because she doesn't want him to see her naked. He doesn't care at what point she is in her bathing. He comes back in and takes everything away, whether she's dressed or not. Then he collects the garbage and stacks the shelves with boxes of cookies and packs of plastic water bottles. That is how Laura knows how much silence separates her from his return: the more food, the more solitude.

* * *

At the beginning, she would count the days. Then she

stopped: they were all the same. She moves slowly. There are scabs on her neck from the collar; the slightest tug and they crack open again. She told him once. He seemed not to hear her. Then he returned with sterilizer and gauze pads. Laura let him dress the wounds. These are the only times he touches her: if he has to put a plaster on her, or brush her forehead to see if she has a fever. While he was attending to her, there was one moment when Laura could have grabbed the scissors and stuck them in his eye. He may well have left them there on the bed, in plain sight, on purpose to bait her. He's always setting up little traps like this. When the little girl passes the test, he grunts with satisfaction. This hurdle was easy; she'd already learned the hard way, after spending days in the toilet stench. Hurting him would only backfire. If this stranger dies, she dies with him. The man has cast an extra-special spell by locking her up. Laura has to pray he won't so much as twist an ankle if she wants to get to the next week.

He brings her presents. Laura only looks at them when the noise has settled down and all that is left is a sensation of deafness, as if everything is wrapped in cotton wool, and the only sound in the room is the hum of the fan. She's careful not to move an inch. The silence that descends on her connects the fleeting breath of light to the solitude she endures for days and days at a time, like a bridge. Keeping the silence going is a game she plays with herself. The longer the bridge stays standing, the greater chance she has of teetering on the brink of the cage without falling in. In the end, though, something always breaks the silence: one of the chain links rattles, or the bedsprings creak . . . the slightest disturbance, and Laura falls headlong into the iron room.

She receives coloring books and reading books. Magazines for girls older than her, with the latest gossip of the love affairs of famous actors and singers. Felt pens, colored pencils, pastels, crayons . . . All things Laura decides not to touch, as she did at first with the food, and still tries to do occasionally. She always loses the battle: the hunger and the thirst are stronger. She goes to the shelf and munches a cookie or sucks a juice carton dry without a thought for her defeat. When he comes back, there is paper and packaging strewn on the floor. He's irritated to find a mess, but he doesn't touch anything. Without so much as glancing at her, he seems to be saying, "Look, you're the one who has to live here." In general, though, he looks contented. Laura has eaten what she's been given. The upright toilet buckets speak clearly of her obedience.

She is similarly defeated by the gifts. Once despair has run its course, minutes are still minutes. Laura comes back down to earth and nothing has shifted. Not even an inch, however much she screams and begs. She yells herself into an exhausted sleep and then opens her eyes with a start, only to begin the cycle again. She can see if it's day or night by pulling the tape off the hole where the cord goes out, but she doesn't do it often, because knowing it's dark outside scares her even more, even though the room stays the same. Then, after hours of despondency, the most incredible thing happens: boredom creeps in. She thinks of it as a flat lake, where nothing ever happens, not even the flicker of a fish or a ripple on the surface of the water. Nothing. That's what she becomes. Sometimes she pushes herself just to raise her heartbeat a little, simply to pass the time of day. To assuage her anxiety, she should sleep, but sleep is not always there waiting. These are the moments when she starts looking at the books.

They are no different from her vacation workbook: join the dots, brainteasers, math problems. She gets hooked on them for a while and thinks of nothing else. She checks the solutions and is outraged if she doesn't get the right answer. The puzzle pages are worn thin with her continuous erasing. She likes the math problems the best, because they keep her company, the wheels in her head turning in the sludge of her brain. If she told the kids at school, they wouldn't believe her.

Every time he leaves, the old scribbled-in books vanish. New ones appear on her desk. This is one of the reasons Laura didn't want to give in, to begin with. Because he's playing the teacher, giving her marks. If she does her lesson well, the next time he brings extra gifts like chocolate or dolls. A new pencil case. One time, Martina.

She's the only one Laura talks to. She has blond braids and eyes that open and close. When Laura pushes a button on her hand, she says "I love you" or "I'm hungry" or "Mamma, please don't leave me." Laura hardly ever pushes that button. The knob that interests Laura is on Martina's breast, under her lilac dress. If you hold it down and speak into it, the doll repeats everything you say, in a disguised voice. Laura sometimes tells Martina stories she invents. Martina tells them back to Laura, in pieces.

She thinks about her parents. She calls out to them as loudly as she can, but the iron wall is so thick it keeps everything inside. When there are storms, the room rocks as if a thousand madmen are pummeling it. The clanging of the iron gets into her bones after a while, making it impossible to work on the brainteasers, or whisper into her new friend's tummy. Laura has to curl up into a ball, covering her ears with her hands, and chant nursery rhymes to herself. With her own voice rumbling in her head, she can keep out the mayhem. Other times, she thinks about her life before she came here. She daydreams so clearly that she drifts into a half-sleep. She revisits precise moments, one of those dinners that turned into an argument for no reason at all—a drop of wine accidentally falling on the tablecloth, say—when the food in her mouth would turn to cement. Then she wakes up from her trance with a jolt, and realizes she is still in the iron room. She is shocked when she realizes she is remembering bad things in order to feel better. It is like a bomb detonating inside her tummy. Especially when she discovers that her mother's face is fading. Her father's is even less distinct; no clearer than a washed-out drawing. Dreaming about them doesn't help. The images continue to fade.

They may still be looking for her. Or maybe they've already given up, seeing that she never came home. In the meantime, the fan has been taken away. She now has two tops to wear, with one pair of pajama bottoms. A thin blanket has also arrived. And some socks, which Laura doesn't put on.

She takes a roll call of her class with the doll, copying her teacher Pina's voice: "Balducci, Boldrini, Canelli, Favilli, Finamore, Giovani, Marchi, Melandri . . . " all the way down to Villoresi, at the end of the alphabet. Martina repeats. Laura closes her eyes and, all of a sudden, comes out with, "Here, Miss!" She envisages the whole scene: her in her school smock at the front of the class, the smell of erasers and fresh pencil sharpenings. Her best friend's face lights up as she looks to her left, where Mirko Tani is fooling around, shooting chewed-up paper cannonballs through an empty Bic pen.

The books that come in are getting harder. Some of the math problems drive her crazy, like the one about the fence:

A farmer needs to fence in his field. Every day, he plants 1 stake while his son plants 3. Every Sunday, a farmer friend plants 2 more (but only on Sundays!). Given that the farmer needs to plant 50 stakes to fence in his field, how many days will it take to complete the task?

The solutions page is no longer there; it gets ripped out before arriving in her room. Now, solving the problems requires a different process. Laura writes a figure and that's what stays. Is it wrong? Is it close? Nobody tells her. The only way she knows is if she finds a jar of Nutella with the Smurfs on it. Or nothing. Instead of apricot juice, she'll have water. If she's been a total dunce, the water won't even be fizzy.

The icy iron wall makes the room colder. Laura wraps a thick woolen scarf under the iron collar and wears three pairs of socks, one on top of the other. On her desk, a little plastic tree with red and blue baubles appears. As well as a wooden advent calendar with numbered drawers. When it arrived, the first two had already been opened, but there was a milk candy inside each one. Laura understood it was December 3. It's beautiful, it feels old and homely. Instead of a crackling fire in the hearth, though, Laura only has an electric fire. She stays so close to it that she practically talks to it. December. If she thinks about it, she feels like she's falling into a gaping abyss. Four months. She's getting desperate. She's also running a fever.

The fever was there, and there was nothing she could do about it. In her delirious state—half-asleep, half-awake, retching and vomiting—at least she was able to see her room at home, her mother at her bedside holding a damp cloth to her forehead. "I had a horrible dream," she would say. Her mother, with the smile she gives her when she's happy says, "Now rest." She opened her eyes. Martina was with her under the blankets that were soaked in sweat. She pushed down on her breast. "You're not alone," the doll said. Laura couldn't even remember saying it.

"Am I going to be staying here forever?" she asked last time he came, as he took stock of what was left on the shelf. He usually writes things down on a pad he takes out of his pocket, as if he were compiling a shopping list of things to bring next time. No answer. "I'm anemic," she said. "Mamma made me drink iron supplements that tasted like rust." He stopped writing, but kept his eyes on the shelf. Then he sighed heavily and wrote something down. He went to the desk, picked up the latest books, and tucked them under his arm. "What's your name? Why are you keeping me here?" He turned on his heels and walked out. A second later, she heard the clang of the deadbolts being pulled down over the door.

Christmas provisions are plentiful: jars, bags of cookies, snacks. Oranges, walnuts, net bags of tangerines. Even a stocking. Water, milk, and orangeade stand side by side in columns on the shelf. Every box that comes in makes Laura's heart leap into her throat. So many days. The only thing that comforts her is the pile of books on the table. The math problems will keep her company. Three packets of batteries, so Martina can carry on talking. And then there's a present with a red ribbon around it.

This time the silent game doesn't last long. As soon as she hears the tires screech on the gravel, she grabs the gift. According to the advent calendar, it's only December 22, but her curiosity gets the better of her. If this is a test to see how long she can wait, she's raised the white flag already.

A blue Walkman. One of the new ones; you don't have to turn the tape around when it finishes. It does it on its own. There's also a radio function. She switches it over, but the iron box insulates her. Reception is almost nonexistent. There's a lot of static, some interference, and occasionally a ghost of a voice that gives her the shivers instead of reassuring her.

There are lots of binders, too. Apart from the usual exercises, there is a collection of *Story Teller* magazines and tapes. Laura opens the first issue, the cassette tape clearly visible behind the plastic. There are two stories to listen to and follow in the magazine: *The Emperor's New Clothes* and *The Pied Piper of Hamelin*. She puts the tape into the Walkman and pushes Play. The fairy-tale music starts and then a voice—the first she has heard in months—takes her breath away. "We need to tell the Emperor, the chancellor cried. There's no more money in the chests . . . " The tears welling up in her eyes make the cage fade a little into the background. Laura picks up the stocking and cuddles up under the blanket with it. She puts a roll of liquorice in her mouth. Martina is lying beside her, her eyes closed. So, Laura closes her eyes, too, while the Emperor complains he can't receive visitors. As he says, he doesn't have a decent thing to wear, even though his wardrobes are bursting. There's no other solution: raise taxes and have a brand-new outfit made.

She pushes Stop and repeats *"My name is"* in English. But it doesn't sound like the woman's voice on the tape. She tries listening to Martina say it back to her. "My name is." She puts the Walkman earphones back in and listens again: "My name is." No way, it's like something from another planet.

All the advent calendar drawers have been open for days. Three days, maybe. Or a hundred. The garbage bin is overflowing. Laura has to push the paper and plastic down into it to get everything in and put the lid on.

Helicopters fly over the container every now and again. Or there's a sonic boom from a low-flying plane. Laura holds her breath. The rumbling moves away, leaving her there on her own. This is one of two ways she knows that outside there's still a world with people in it. The other is the radio. She's worked out that, from the bottom corner of her bed, she can find a frequency that picks up a signal, even though the static is still strong, and the voices break up like crackling robots. She needs to stay completely still; a sneeze is enough to lose all contact. There's only one battery left on her desk. She likes listening to the tapes, but it uses up a lot of power.

The radio programs are full of talk. There's the news, too. When the signature tune comes on, she feels a blow to the stomach. "They might talk about me," she thinks but they never do. She hears traffic updates for the Great Ring Road (she's never heard of it), yogurt commercials, and phone-ins from listeners. Silvia from Florence, Gianni from Bari (where's that?). People who really exist, who are speaking at the same time as she's listening. She can't wait for the songs. Martina looks at her disapprovingly. Her big blue eyes rebuke her for not being more disciplined, warning her she'll be sentenced to a life of silence if she isn't. It's the same with food. She often eats out of boredom. She'd gotten through the bottles of orangeade a while ago, and she hasn't touched the water for days. It may be an impression, but she feels the collar is tighter than it was before. Martina tells her, without actually saying it, "It's like in that fairy tale. One day they'll come and get you, all fattened up, and roast you on the spit. That's why you're here."

"I am. You are. He is. She is. We are . . ." It sounds like a prayer, a mantra she's repeated so many times it's lost its meaning.

Two days have gone by since the storm. She knows this because she's been checking the hole with the cord from the lamp through it. No headphones, no Martina. Moving around in the dark is like not moving at all. The chains rattle, and Laura's worst nightmare is tripping over her toilet buckets and filling the room with the stench of her piss and shit again. She gropes her way to the shelf and fumbles around among the packets of food. There's nothing left. Even the jam is finished. She may even be dead already and she wouldn't know it. The darkness and silence are so intense that they make her feel like a ghost. And yet, her real terror is that she's stopped thinking about her parents. When she realizes it, she takes a deep breath. She's split in two, like when she's sunbathing at the beach and suddenly gets hit by a water bomb. She persists, searching her memory for scenes from her past that she once clung to as precious. But she soon gets bored. Her mind is already somewhere else. A completely different place made of nothingness: just her breathing, her presence there. She's been through the fear; she's wept all her tears. That's enough, now. She knows nothing about anything. She feels her way back, bumping into things dopily. She's in a trance, existing without existing. The screeching of the tires sounds like it's coming from another dimension, as does the clanking of the deadbolts. The white rectangle opens up wide, letting in sunshine and icy air. The light catches her out. She thought she was somewhere else in the room. The first things she feels is a discharge of pins pricking her body from head to toe. Then she opens her mouth and sucks in the air as if she's been breathing through a straw until this point. When she looks at her hands, she doesn't recognize them. She has the sensation of watching them crumble into dust on the spot.

Gian Burrasca: A Bad Boy's Diary, The Adventures of Pinocchio, Treasure Island. A new story has arrived: *The Baron in the Trees.* Martina has listened to the whole thing, from beginning to end. She says, "Again." So, Laura reads the book again.

He looks at her flopping on the bed, dispirited and whiny. He's an old man, and he may even feel a little sympathy for her, though he keeps her chained up like an animal. She's lost heart, become discouraged. She can't keep going. Laura clings onto Martina and watches the man scratching at the door. When he came in, the wind had slammed the door shut behind him with a thud. The thump she usually hears had taken place this time with him inside. She watches him blaming himself for his mistake, struggling with the massive iron door. He's panting and muttering things the little girl doesn't understand.

You've gotten yourself trapped inside the cage you made for me. How does it feel? Laura thinks. He takes his glasses off. The man whimpers, like a little animal. From the other end of the container, it's almost funny. All of a sudden, in a fit of anger, he bangs his fist against the metal plating. He drops to the floor, his back against the door, and turns out his pockets. In his palm he produces a few coins and a key; she can't see what else. They are no help. He looks over the supplies: nothing is missing, the buckets have been emptied. Laura shifts her weight and inadvertently touches the knob on the doll's breast. Her whiny voice echoes around the big room: "I love you."

It is clear. Nobody will be coming to save them. Her prayers have been answered halfway: the man will die, but so will she. She decides right there and then; she won't shed a single tear.

She refuses to speak to him, and it feels like a weapon. It's good to realize she's better prepared for disaster than he is. She sees him taking shallow breaths, trying to take back control. He doesn't give up. Holding onto the ridges between the iron plates, he pulls himself to his feet. He studies the doorjamb and the hinges. He tries forcing the door open in various places with his shoulders. It doesn't give. His groans make little white clouds. He snorts something like "Holy Christ . . . " Laura catches a glimpse of his wedding ring. He's married. Is the wife alive? Does she know what her husband is doing? Are there any children? What are their names? Maybe there's someone out there waiting for him, too.

It's a performance she's never seen before. Laura watches from her bed, as if she were at the movies. The man takes his jacket off and puts it on the little cupboard at the entrance, where the little girl cannot reach because her chain is too short. He's wearing a nice shirt. He unbuttons the cuffs and, despite the cold, rolls his sleeves up over his elbows. He loosens his tie, as if he were having difficulty breathing. He needs to think. Then he looks deflated: there are no cracks or handholds. Maybe Laura should start yelling like she did on the first day, punching the wall with her bare knuckles, slamming her head against the iron sheeting to help her sleep. Instead, she is calm. For once, she lets him be the one to be devoured by monsters.

She is one of them. The idea of picking him to the bone with her silence makes her mouth water. The man hides his face with his hands, his shoulders shuddering. He is so scared, he looks crazy. When he takes his hands away, she sees he's not crying. Rather, he's laughing out loud. Laura wonders what people will find in a hundred years. He carries on laughing, a deep belly laugh. Then, with a masterful sleight of hand, the door opens with its usual creaking sound. The evening light floods the cage.

He tidies himself up, buttons up his cuffs, and adjusts his tie. Calmly. He even starts whistling. He puts his jacket on and combs his hair back with his hands. Then he collects her workbooks and sticks them under his arm. The show is over. His experiment has given him results. Now Laura knows two things. First, if need be, she's willing to let herself die without making a fuss. Second, the man is meaner than she thought.

Martina Cancelli is living her everyday life, back home in 167 West. Her heart misses a beat when Mirko Tani walks down the corridor at recess. Laura wonders who her new best friend is. Maybe that bitch Melandri, her face splattered with freckles. Laura is traveling elsewhere, diving headlong into the adventures of Tom Sawyer and Oliver Twist. She is experiencing the burning emotions of the March sisters; sitting at a desk with Bottini and his classmates in the novel *Heart*. The world as she knows it is enclosed in this room, on the shelf that appeared at the end of the winter.

There are 23 English lesson tapes, 26 *Story Teller* collections, and four music cassettes. There's also an atlas with maps that open out onto two or three pages. She knows where Mississippi is; Alaska looks like a patch of land kissing Siberia. Sometimes she shows them to the doll. "Look, this is where I come from," she says pointing. But she doesn't know where they are now.

She reads out loud. It lets her know she's still alive, though that has become a vague concept. She listens on the radio to the same songs her friends would be listening to after doing their homework. They are all quite cheesy, especially the Italian ones: love, love, and more love. The English songs are more fun. Laura gets a kick when she manages to understand some of the words she has learned from the woman's voice on the tapes. She picks them out in the English children's books she has been brought, which she reads a lot, pronouncing the words carefully: *Around the World in 80 Days* or *Shark in the Park*, which has lovely pictures. *Bedtime Stories for Little Children* sometimes takes her breath away. Then *Lord of the Rings* arrived.

In the old days, her prizes were cookies or candies. Now she asks for books. Laura completes her assignments in a flash, knowing full well there will be no need for the red pen in her notebooks. In exchange, she gets *The Sword of Shannara*, *The Magic Kingdom of Landover*, *Firestarter*. Martina listens to them at night, her eyes wide open.

All they talk about on the radio these days is the Pope's Jubilee. In two days, it will be Easter: April 23. That means in exactly one week it will be her birthday. She doesn't want to think about it. She picks up her notebook and starts working on her history and geography essays. Math is still her weak point, but she can't do anything about it. Her brain just doesn't seem to work like that. She is never punished for it, though. On the contrary, he brings books about other subjects. A new issue of the magazine *The Great Civilizations of the Ancient World*, for example.

Laura knows what she is working for: something to soothe her solitude. Sometimes she feels like a trained monkey, constantly preparing for an exam that never comes. She should be in her own room with Martina Cancelli, dressing and undressing Barbie dolls, but here she is writing a two-page summary of the expansion of the Assyrians as they conquered Babylon, Anatolia, Jerusalem, and Egypt. Why does she need to know all this stuff? Because it's her only way of making sure the new episode of the *Chronicles of Dragonlance* will get to her, or of finding out what happens next to Lyra Silvertongue, as she follows her father into an alternate universe . . .

* * *

The anatomy text book says it's perfectly normal: the lining of the uterus sheds through the vagina, you can't die from it. Progesterone and estrogen levels drop sharply when there is no implantation, resulting in thick brown blood that looks like poster paint. When she got up, Laura thought she had pooped: the cramps are the same as the times she has had to get the lids off the toilet buckets in a hurry. It may be normal, but it's still disgusting. She's embarrassed to put her dirty panties in the laundry basket; she doesn't know why. It feels private.

The radio gives snippets of news here and there. It's June 9. Clementina Cantoni has been freed 24 days after being kidnapped. Negotiations are under wraps; the Afghanis deny a ransom was ever paid. Laura denies the evidence, too. She has to use drinking water to wash herself, and pours some Coca-Cola onto the dirty towel, rubbing hard to get rid of the stain. She wets the cloth, rubs, wets it again. But the stink won't go away. She gives up and leaves everything down there. Let whatever is supposed to happen, happen. She says to Martina, "Today I've become a woman." Martina looks at her as if to say, "Bad luck."

In the world outside, bombs go off; trains, streets, and buildings are blown up. The newspapers he brings write about terrorist attacks, violence, and oppression. She remembers when it was normal to go out shopping without fearing for your life. If you believe the front-page news, it sounds like nowadays you risk being knifed. Laura is safe. She's fourteen, and she's grown up overnight, even though she's locked in an iron box. Like the flower that has grown in a corner of the container. It found a chink and thrust its way through; it was not held back by the metal casing. That's how living things function. Maybe she should do the same: find a chink, and thrust her way through it.

There are good and bad people outside. Laura learns this from the block-capital headlines. Political debates make her yawn, but she reads every inch of the paper anyway. She has no idea what some of the words mean: "reform" or "amendment," for example. She looks up the words in her dictionary, then checks the English equivalent.

Of all the revolutions she's read about, the one she likes the most is called the Internet. She's not sure what it is, but she does know people go crazy over it. Some experts say it's a fad that will soon pass; others say the world will never be the same again. There are lots of new words to look up: "browser," "link," "homepage," "email" . . . However hard Laura racks her brain, she can't fathom what Web 2.0 refers to. Nor can she make head or tail of expressions like SMS, GSM, WAP, "roaming" and "handover" for cell phones. Something big is happening, other than the regular shoot-outs. She still loves reading *The Master and Margarita* and *Harry Potter*, but the real world outside is being turned upside-down, and she's only brushing the surface. Theory is no longer enough. As he's about to leave, Laura says, "I want a computer."

At the last minute, after he's done the weekly clean and picked up the bag of dirty laundry, Laura says, "I changed last night."

The words seem to make him gag. He coughs a little and then he closes the door.

The electric cord has broken. For a moment, Laura thinks she's destined to eternal darkness, even though she handed in her paper on Australia on time. But she soon sees that the cord has been transformed into a double socket. Then the boxes arrive.

Assembling it takes no time at all: there's a metal tower, a screen, and a keyboard. In addition, there's a gadget the instruction booklet calls a "mouse" in both English and Italian.

With something that looks like a TV, the iron room feels different. All of a sudden, it has been transformed into the cabin of a spaceship. Laura looks at the machine without touching it. She knows what a "bit" is, and understands binary programming language. Reading about Vannevar Bush's memex device was like science fiction for her, and now here is his imagined memory supplement reduced to 20 pounds. In his day, a calculator occupied a giant cage bigger than this one. That is called "hardware." Laura leafs through the thick instruction manual and feels like she's reading the machine's soul. Which, in computers, is called "software."

Operative system, file manager, programming language, graphic user interface. A new world made up of floppy disks and CD-ROMS. The message she has received, as usual in total silence, is that from now on her assignments should be done on the computer. No more notebooks. Instead of books, Laura receives flat plastic boxes filled with the silver discs she had already come across in newspapers and magazines a good while back. She looks at her reflection in them and doesn't recognize herself. Especially now that her hair has been cut. She looks like a boy.

There's a port in the CPU for her headphones, replacing the Walkman for everything except the radio. As well as English and French, there's a new language to learn called MS-DOS. You ask a question, and the computer answers, searching and finding the information. "We're not alone anymore," she says to Martina. The doll's eyes shine.

The command DIR conjures up a list of files and subdirectories in a directory. The command SET visualizes, imposes, or removes environment variables of cmd.exe. When she tries the prompt SC for Service Control, she is told the order is not recognized. Martina says, "Can we create some precise requests?" Asking is important. It defines you. It's an identity badge.

Playing Solitaire and Minesweeper occupies days at a time. Hours that feel like minutes. "One more match," Laura says out loud, while her homework assignments pile up. In fact, *The Dark Tower II* does not get delivered. In recompense, she has acquired a third hand, having learned to point the cursor as quick as a flash.

Writing her assignments with TXT is fun. It feels like she's creating pages in a real book. Her first experiment is a paper on an Amazonian tribe. It sounds impossible, but there is a tribe that has no idea of the passage of time. She is so jealous of them, with no need for clocks. The tribe is called the Amondawa. They were first discovered in 1986, hidden in the middle of a boundless forest in the heart of Brazil. Months and years mean nothing to them. They only know four numbers, and make do with them for everything they need. There are only two things they care about: whether it's raining or whether it's not. Birthdays and calendars don't exist. In the first part of your life you are given one name and in the second, another. When the chieftain was asked to translate the word "time" into his language, his answer was "sun."

The CD-ROMs she has been left are encyclopedias. Windows onto the world. Narrative voices. Laura sticks white labels on the floppy disks and writes in felt pen which of the projects she has completed is saved there. The most surprising thing is that Visual Basic has made math much easier, too;

she'd been struggling with it for a while. The exercises stimulate a different part of her brain. Laura has learned how to burn CDs and program DirectPlay. She loves playing around with the dynamic arrays. Whereas before, her math problems involved calculating how long a farmer would take to build a fence, now the exercises set for her—to be worked out on paper, without the aid of the computer—sound more or less like this:

> When debugging application IIS in Visual Basic the program IE opens, with the error message "404 Page Not Found." This is because IIS is managed by W2000 and the reference to the file local host is different for VB and IIS W2000. How would you modify the reference?

And she's good at it.

Some videos have arrived: documentaries and college lectures. For Laura this is worse than a punch to the gut. There he is, sitting at a desk, a blue panel behind him. At the beginning of every lecture, after the theme tune, there is a banner with the words, "Cultural Anthropology, Ethnology, Ethnolinguistics." Underneath, "Carlo Maria Balestri."

The first thing she notes is that this is the proof. There he is, talking to Laura on a screen. No, he's talking to a plural *you* as if there were a class of students in front of him. The man who keeps her locked up in this iron cage, therefore, cultivates young people, boys and girls, for whatever reason. How many iron boxes are there? She thought she was the chosen one. She was wrong. From the computer screen the man says, "Welcome everybody to the third lesson of . . . " Welcome *everybody*. The idea that there are others like her offends her.

The second thing she notes is the name: he has taken off his mask and this is fatal. It speaks a thousand words. In a hidden corner of herself, Laura had still hoped she would wake up one day having been dumped with no clothes on at the side of a street. Now she can forget it. She knows what he looks like. Moreover, she would be able to look him up. If he hadn't been completely sure she would be held here forever, he certainly wouldn't have risked revealing himself.

The third thing she notes is the voice: it's sweet, like a grandfather's. He smiles occasionally, especially when he cracks a joke. And he has a funny tic—continuous little sniffs—that punctuates the flow of his words, especially when he warms to his subject. Laura doesn't listen to a word of the content; she studies the man. His cold blue eyes that she can never really focus on here in the cage. His thin, grey mustache. His hands. He rests them on the desk, palms down, as if they were detached from his body. It's absurd: at every lecture, he's wearing a different colored bow tie, but the jacket is always the same. Completely different from the clothes he wears when he comes into the cage.

Finally, the fourth thing she notes is that the whole thing may be a setup, yet another test she is required to take. Laura can picture him setting up a video camera, tinkering with the theme tune, the banner, and the welcome. The plural *you* that is really just for her. Martina asks her, "Have we gone up a level?"

It's four-thirty P.M. No accidents on the Great Ring Road in Rome. Not much traffic on the Milan bypass. A stopped vehicle in the lane heading east: pay attention to debris in the road. Laura switches the radio off when a soppy Italian song about love, love, and more love comes on.

At times, like now, Laura can't get Martina Cancelli's face out of her head. It disgusts her to admit it, but the image is clear, while that of her parents is just a distant aura. Even in her dreams, their faces are indistinct. On rare occasions, she manages to catch hold of them but then, when she wakes up, they have already vanished beyond the horizon of the desert she has inside of her. Her eyelids open onto the iron walls of the room and—poof!—they are gone. And yet, her best friend's pony-tail is branded onto her memory. Because all this is Martina's fault.

Laura spends whole days speaking to her over the rattling of her chain. "I came out to meet you, and you left me on my own," she snaps in her doll's face. "Look where I am now." The doll's face is the same as her blood sister's. The pact between them never really existed, which should have served as a warning. One morning, they're in their corner of the park, on the roundabout. The idea of joining their destinies forever leads them to break one of the empty bottles they always find there. Laura doesn't hesitate; she slices into her thumb pad until shiny red blood gushes out. "It's your turn." Martina Cancelli picks up the shard of glass and turns it around in her hands, while Laura's blood has already formed a dark pool in her palm. "Come on!" Her best friend uses the glass to scrape the mud out of her nails. A drop of Laura's blood drips onto the strap of her sandals. "If we don't mix it together, the pact doesn't count." Martina Cancelli walks in a circle, partly enjoy-ing the scene and partly more terrified than even she ever imagined she would be. She looks as if she's about to cut her-self but it's all a performance. She shows Laura the scratch on the tip of her thumb, while Laura's blood is dripping onto the back of her hand (she's already anemic, so she's feeling weak). "You need to cut deeper," Laura says. Martina Cancelli takes a deep breath and makes another attempt. It hurts. She plonks herself down on the roundabout, which creaks a little with her weight. Her eyes glaze over. "Are you blacking out?" Laura asks her, recognizing herself in her friend's vacant stare, even though she has no idea what she looks like when she faints. Her friend grins stupidly and holds out her thumb: Laura understands that's the best she can do. The best people can do is enough, even when people expect more of them. Her father once told her that there were some people who found getting out of the house a really big deal. He said that when they succeed, they should be encouraged and respected. So, Laura respects Martina Cancelli, who can't give her more than a superficial scratch. She presses the tip of her thumb that is drenched in blood onto Martina's dry thumb pad and says, "Now we are like sisters." Martina Cancelli stares at her with a girlish simper. Her friend's bloodied hand makes her feel faint. She nods and then pulls her finger away, gets up, and heads off in a hurry toward home. "Like sisters!" Laura shouts behind her. Martina Cancelli, head down, keeps walking while blood continues to drip from Laura's hand.

The Red and the Black makes her feel weak at the knees; *Anna Karenina* breaks her heart. Laura reads relentlessly, even in the icy cold when her hands are numb. There are moments when she sees an invisible thread weaving around the iron room connecting everything together: it starts from the asteroids and Hurrian tattoo motifs, and weaves through Alice's adventures in Wonderland, laser printers, and the first steps on the moon. They are special but fleeting moments. One second, the whole picture is lit up; the next, she's plunged into darkness and has to work hard to figure out the overall design from a fragment. It's like trying to catch a comet by the tail: in the time it takes to look at your hands, it is already millions of miles away. All that's left is the smell of burning flesh.

Laura had never seen her mother reading a book. Her father used to like checking the soccer results in the newspaper in the café at 167 West. These are the abysmal freeze frames she carries with her. Hegel would say there is nothing deeper than what appears on the surface. "What about me, then?" Laura asks herself, without ever finding the answer.

She had been a normal, well-behaved little girl. Before the

abduction, the worst thing she ever did was steal an eraser from Agostino's stationery store, which a couple of years later was emptied out and turned into a tobacco store. For a while, she was convinced she had contributed to the stationer's demise. She often thought it was her theft that had left him bankrupt. Self-made people, who had made their way by dint of hard work, were left on the streets thanks to light-fingered Laura. Agostino and Miranda were out of work, eating out of cans in their old age. Everyone in the neighborhood knew it.

There was another time, with the praying mantises. Michele Paini had brought two of them—a male and a female—into class one day, each in their own jar. The female had two black spots on her front legs that looked like eyes. The whole class was spellbound during that lesson, because they were learning about their mating habits: the female bites off the male's head and devours his corpse for nutrition, while his genitals continue to deliver sperm. Even though half of his body has been munched through, the male doesn't stop. During recess, Laura secretly opened the jars and put the two revolting creatures together. It was a bloodbath.

The time with the turtles was just a game. Mirko Tani had brought three soft-shelled turtles to school. They were like little sponges. He kept them in a shoebox and was incredibly possessive over them. Laura had taken one and hid it in her pocket. When Mirko noticed it had gone, there was a skirmish among the boys in the class. He blamed Staccioli immediately, because he was always stealing snacks and pencils; once he even tried to pinch the teacher's fountain pen. The boys tried to get their hands into the pocket of his school smock, but he slithered out of their reach like a snake and threatened to beat up anyone who came close. That afternoon, Laura built a little enclosure out of stones in her garden and let Clementina roam. She fed her lettuce leaves and carrot sticks and told her parents she'd found her in the park. The turtle felt right at home in less than a week. But then her birthday came around, and Mirko Tani was invited to the party. Laura only remembered about the turtle when she saw him walk through the gate. So as not to be found out, she ran to the garden, picked the little thing up, and dropped it into one of the holes in a brick her mother had used to line the path to protect her precious mimosa and lemon trees. She didn't pull Clementina out of the hole until later that evening once the party was over. The turtle was covered in ants, and her eyes had been eaten away.

This is the sum total of her sins. Laura has been trapped like Clementina. She stole an eraser, and now her whole life is going to be erased. An animal is eating away at her day by day. It's called solitude. She pays her mother's and father's debts: they never read books. She devours hundreds of them. These are her punishments.

* * *

The whole point of Facebook is to control everybody. It's a place where you can shout to the world ten times a day that you exist, even when you live in a cupboard under the stairs. Other solitudes answer with a smiley face. It gets everywhere. Even the bathroom. *Especially* the bathroom. The guy who founded the empire of the ego is a zillionaire.

The tablet has no connection to the internet. The contents are carefully dosed: videos, songs, e-books. Laura watches the global revolution unfold from a room that could well be dug deep into the center of the earth. The exercises on algorithms and advanced offline programming keep her awake.

Write a recursive function that receives as a parameter an integer N then generate and visualize onscreen all the binary numbers in a bit.

Martina says, "*Include <stdio.h>.*"

She says, "*Void binaryNumberIte (int.n).*"

It's the DNA of a new world. Flow charts, instances, variables, pseudocodes, and iterations. Hieroglyphics, the Punic Wars, ogival or Gothic arches, Modigliani: everything is there, in a structure of complex data that dominates life today. Even paying for 8 ounces of sausage descends from an array.

In the meantime, newspapers report the big leap forward: Facebook is reported on Wall Street as one of the highest initial public offerings ever to take place. On the first day, the stock set a new record for trading volume, and the company's value skyrocketed to $104 billion. They've bought Instagram. They'll soon be buying WhatsApp. Traffic in data is gold. Judging by the magazines she reads, Laura imagines Martina Cancelli can't live without taking selfies and sharing them with the rest of the world as she gets ready for a Saturday night.

Laura does it, too. The tablet captures her with a chain around her neck and her hair combed back, as if a carload of friends is about to pass by 167 West, pick her up, and go out to a nightclub. The doll fakes her mother's voice, "Be good. Don't trust strangers." Parents are such a drag.

Laura takes a Camel cigarette out of the pack and lights it. She has to ration them, or she goes crazy when there are none left. The first pack stayed on her desk unopened for weeks before she made up her mind. Her mother smoked, too. After making ends meet in her room (she would have made more money if she'd created an online yearbook, but books were never her thing). By the time Laura realized it was yet another trap, it was too late. The habit had already gotten into her blood: a new way to keep her in the cage, induce her to meet her deadlines, and persuade her to give her utmost. Her prizes have come down to this: nicotine. Her days have become a struggle; her eyes wander from the screen to the pack. She must resist, keep her focus. It's not losing her chocolate rations, or her stacks of adventure stories, that worries her now; it's the head-spinning satisfaction of the first puff, like in the films. When her supply of cigarettes is getting low, she starts chewing her nails. The slightest sound makes her look over toward the door in case he's on his way. Eventually, the door actually opens. It's him. He brings food and drink. Books. Laura watches him from her bed, gauging his every movement. The man is a sadist. He waits until the last minute. Sometimes he pretends to forget until he's at the door, when she's already rearing up in desperation. "Hey!" Only then does he put his hand in his pocket. He pulls out a handful of cigarettes, counts them one by one, and lines them up by the keyboard. They're like a killer's bounty. Six, seven, eight . . . He stops. "More!" Laura shouts, from the other end of the container. Nine . . . no, eight. He picks one back up again and turns on his heels. "Please!" Nothing. The clang of the iron door shutting sends its message: "If you want more, study more."

Saturday night, though, when she's completed all her assignments, she loves imagining herself at a party. With deafening music in her headphones plugged into the computer, she twirls and turns in her pajama bottoms, pulling the cord as far as it will go. She doesn't hear the rattling of the chain. Her eyes closed, she blows smoke into the air fantasizing that she is in the middle of a crowd of boys watching her goof around. One of them touches her.

The title is straightforward: *Community Symbols: An Essay in Cultural Anthropology*. It's a big, thick, serious-looking book that Laura found near the computer after his last visit. It says *Carlo Maria Balestri* on the cover. But she is the real author.

Many of her assignments—corrected, edited, and rewritten—have ended up in the book. Digressions based on the ideas she had in the iron room without knowing what purpose they served. She doesn't know whether to consider the book a trophy or a slap in the face.

Is this his way of allowing her out? A few moments of yard time afforded by all those pages that concealed screams nobody would ever hear. Well, her mother and father certainly won't hear them. For all she knows, they've already replaced her with a new baby, who might go to college one day and read this book written by his cooped-up jailbird sister and never even know it. It's a cruel game the man is playing. And yet, Laura feels as though she has taken some oxygen into her lungs. She is speaking to the outside world. Even better; she's teaching them. She's educating people by pointing out the changes that have taken place out there. She, of all people. What stuns Laura the most is the price tag. There's a bar code that identifies it, which means that Laura is being chosen. Bought. In the jacket blurb, it says the author belongs to the Prometheus Society, which only accepts members with exceptionally high IQs: from the 99th percentile of the population upwards. She must be one of them.

* * *

Encoding her assignments is fun. The hardest part is making sure it's flawless. The text must be copied and pasted almost entirely, in the hope that he won't notice the contents. She writes every paper in a different language: English, French, or Spanish. The intervals between the letters are fixed, and the message is always the same. "Help. Carlo Maria Balestri is holding me prisoner." Every 3,000 characters, including spaces. All she needs is a bright student to see the pattern. Or some brilliant researcher whose curiosity might be triggered, wondering whether the academic bigwig's latest article was a prank of some kind.

Professor Balestri needs fresh blood to replenish his tired-out mind after all those years of research, and Laura's hard work provides him with the pages he needs. She knows how he writes, his linguistic tics, his idiolect. For example, he detests adverbs. Apart from a few, which he uses assiduously in his video lectures: evidently, formally, exclusively. His treatises are peppered with semicolons, which give him great satisfaction. He loves provocative digressions, and subtle irony is his signature. He finds cynicism deplorable (of course he does; a man as intelligent as he is). He lives in the midst of it, but the world is becoming confusing, even for him. Laura's intuitions on contemporary life are the ones he ransacks in particular, and these are the tracts where she plants her pleas for help. Because she is completely cut off from the world, it is as if she were observing it from the porthole of a spaceship. But, in fact, she lives and breathes on Gaia, and has a telepathic relationship with plants, animals, mountains, and oceans . . . She may be in an iron box, but she is playing an active role on the outside. Now, more than ever, because she has surpassed him. Carlo Maria Balestri learns from her the potential of MS-DOS, the implications of a digital existence, and the new language of TV series. Her tasks are now: "Read this. Watch this. Tell me what it means, where it fits." She does all her homework and gets Season 4 of *Breaking Bad* in reward, in addition to two packs of Camels. The cigarettes are what keep her one step ahead.

The man grows increasingly confident. Laura's articles start circulating and create quite a stir. His reputation goes from strength to strength. Professor Balestri has found himself a personal trainer, who helps him stay in the spotlight rather than dwindle and fade toward retirement (some of his colleagues proudly boast they still write their papers in pen and have their secretaries type them out). He can hardly take issue with an article where she discusses Pearl Jam and the burden of a certain cultural revolution, in relation to the meager aspirations of contemporary youth, mutilated by their enthusiasm for an app that tells them when they should drink a glass of water. Newspapers become an important outlet; Laura interprets the storms he has lost sight of. When she stops, he stops. Who is holding whom in a cage? In exchange, she asks for more cigarettes, as well as the latest book by DeLillo, or *Born Villain*. A few days later, she finds everything on the table. She writes a three-page piece on the renewed cognitive structure of a society grasping at straws, which receives a standing ovation. The great master never loses his touch; his view of the world is unique. The article is announced on the front page. The girl's call for help is clearly visible. But nobody comes.

* * *

Words fly off the keyboard and land on the screen like raindrops. "Finishing Jubilee Street" has been on a loop all afternoon in her earbuds. The thumping of a pick ax in her earphones. A new article by the scientist who opens up new horizons—while having none herself—will be yet another success in the regular column: *A Word to Young People*. The topics are Google Glass, robots with a high level of consciousness (self-programming is expected to be complete by 2026, just thirteen years away), and the slow activities conducted by Karnak priests who come down from the sacred lake every day to clean the temple of the debris of the night before. The dangers of speed. The value of slowness, of simple, mindful gestures. If the boring old farts want to read this stuff, she can dish it up.

There's a gust of fresh air, like every time he comes: the door is open. Laura doesn't even turn around; she keeps her eyes glued to the screen. She stubs out her last-but-one cigarette; there's thick smoke in the room. Then something that has never happened before takes place—she feels a human touch. The police officer is more shocked than the girl. He speaks to her while the others in his patrol explore the container. Not that there's much to explore.

Laura thinks, "My messages have been received." The music still crashing in her ears, Laura raises her voice and shouts, "Just a minute. I need to finish up here."

THE THIRD FACE

L aura eats everything. We pour her some water and she says, "Thank you." Pointing to the vegetable stew she asks, "Is there any more?" and I run into the kitchen.

Daniele has taken it quite well, but he's worried. We lie next to each other in bed for hours in the evening, staring at the ceiling. The house is immersed in silence, but it still speaks: there's an alien presence that makes the room feel as though it's suspended midair. At times, I just go ahead and say it: "She's still my daughter." It sounds weird, as if I have to convince myself before anyone else. He holds out his hand, looking for mine, and squeezes it. It's his way of saying that everything will be fine. He's here. He's holding on. He wasn't prepared, but he's holding on.

It's like winning the lottery backwards. I lost a little girl of eight, and I've gotten her back at 22. She asked permission to step into the house. We looked into each other's eyes, and our worlds had to reconfigure. I recognized her immediately. Then I fainted.

The therapist says it'll take time.

After fourteen years, more time.

* * *

The neighbors stare inquiringly at this girl who has arrived out of the blue. We are forced to invent stories. The rules are clear: in this building, I'm Laura's auntie. We mustn't attract unwanted attention.

As I told him my story, Daniele's big boyish eyes were killing me. He kept interrupting me, "And so . . . And so . . . " Yes, I had a secret, all right. A little girl who'd been abducted. "And in all these years . . . ?" No, I never had the courage to tell him. It was a way of forgetting, maybe. A way to heave myself forward. The first time he saw me I was just me, with that dark secret, my wrecked face weathered by the wind. Little did he know that I was teetering on the brink of a gaping chasm, and that I'd never walked away from the edge. Our conversations about having kids, even though we were a little past it. My reluctance couched in recklessness: "Let's enjoy life; kids are tough nuts to crack," followed by a suggestion of a trip to India, instead. Or America, Africa, Mars. Anything to postpone the discussion. My biological clock ticking away. "Our friends all have teenagers who are giving them hell." I said that quite a bit, even though I felt I was falling backwards.

At times, I would find him at the computer, logged onto his home banking. He would be staring at that pile of cash he'd made after selling his penthouse apartment in Corso Venezia, close to a subway stop. "What should I do with this money," he seemed to be saying. I would observe his yearning as he watched a 30-year-old father lift a bundled-up baby out of a pram, and I'd distract him by pointing out something in a store window. Then, one evening, there's a knock on the door. Laura is back.

It was him who picked me up. Every morning, as he came down the stairs, he would say, "Good morning," as I fumbled with the mop and pails of water, dressed in the cleaning company's blue uniform. And I would say, "Good morning," back. Some days, I could hardly stand up. I was ashamed of my state. Before going to work, I would squeeze a lemon, add a teaspoon of salt and a half-cup of espresso, and swill it down with 30 drops of Valium. After work, back in my apartment in Via Gracchi, I would go back to the bottle. Two rooms, a bathroom, a kitchenette. And a bed, where I ended up entertaining guys of all shapes and sizes. Who cared if they were good-looking or not? As long as they provided recreational substances. Then I would give them what they came for.

It's not easy looking at yourself in the mirror when you're nearly forty, and realizing you are taking revenge on life by slowly destroying yourself. It's the only pleasure you get. You seek it. It hurts you, and, out of spite, you want it to be even more painful. You look at your reflection, and ask, "Where are you going with this?" Your existence is killing you, and you let it suffer with you, your heart wide open. "Eat me, if you have the courage. You have to be the one to do it." Scratches and burns during the crying fits. Tears are the real enemy, it's like ceding ground. When they start flowing, anger takes over. Alcohol does the rest. Drugs do the rest. Waking up is the worst: the apartment is a battleground, there are bruises all over you. You have no memory of why your pillow is lying, ripped open, on the other side of the room. Or why you are still alive. You go up to the mirror and spit at it. The reflection is enough. Dark drops fall into the washbasin. Concealer is useful, but it can't work miracles. "Good morning," Daniele says one morning. "Good morning," I answer, sunglasses on, curved over the mop. My stomach sinks when I hear steps coming toward me. I can no longer avoid looking up. I lift my head. He doesn't say anything. My split lip speaks for both of us. I'm trembling. Silence bears down on us, as heavy as the building. His first real words to me are, "This can't go on. They can't keep doing this to you." I curse myself, but I can't stop. I burst into tears. In that unflattering pose, with a mop in my hand.

Milan was a random choice; I could have ended up anywhere. The same for Marco. Having a daughter who vanishes
into thin air puts any relationship through the meat grinder,
even one made in heaven. Ours, which had been held together
with spit, hadn't stood a chance in hell. One evening, five years
ago, I walked into the living room after dinner. The TV was on,
and Daniele was waiting for me to watch a new episode of I
don't remember which series. I cuddled up next to him on the
sofa. My ex-husband had just died in a car crash. I didn't say a
word. I'd heard it in the most sordid way possible: from
Facebook.

Donà is not just a lawyer to Daniele; he's an old friend and
has been a companion on many adventures, both inside and
outside the courthouse. After almost half a century, they still
call one another by their last names. It's what people do in
Milan. Salvatore informed us immediately: the latest profiles
confirm that one of the features of the man who had kept
Laura segregated for 14 years was that he chose little girls with
parents from a medium to low socioeconomic background,
who were isolated from their communities. It was his way of
protecting himself: limited connections, little or no resources,
no rich granddaddy with the means to move mountains and
fund ongoing searches. Marco and I couldn't have known it,
but the day we made our first promise to one another in that
attic room in Via Buozzi, thus becoming penniless and
uprooted, was the day we sealed our daughter's fate.

I didn't attend the funeral. A part of me attends his funeral
every day. Marco tried really hard. Remembering his loving
gaze when Laura was a little girl is one of the things that's kept
me alive. When I was at rock bottom, I would sometimes snug-
gle down in a memory bathed in a unique shade of blue, and
linger there. It was hard, but it was our life. Going out for a
pizza was an exceptional event. We celebrated the day we

managed to snag a thirty-year mortgage. We were being stran-
gled by a loan that would kill us, but we still drank to our good
fortune, overflowing with love, gazing into each other's eyes.
These are the goals of normal people. A little sad, a little overwhelming. "She has your jawline," he would say. Diamonds
were worth nothing compared to those words, the way he said
them. I would surprise myself unexpectedly thinking that
moments like those were what life was all about. A few years
later, we were in the kitchen tearing our hair out, hundreds of
cigarettes stubbed out in our glasses. Laura had disappeared
just over a week before. The devil's tongue lay between us,
licking so ruthlessly that our bones were picked clean. Without
our daughter, we were no longer enough for each other. There
had already been a number of landslides that eroded the once
solid mountain of our love. Our pain was a pool of tar that was
drowning us, and we could do nothing to keep our heads
above the surface. When he went back to doing extra shifts, I
took it as an insult. It was like starting over again. I knew the
bank didn't accept late payments, regardless of family
tragedies. The manager had said, "We understand there's been
a slight problem, but . . . " A slight problem.

Nobody ever thought there'd be a ransom. Right from day
one, the most likely scenario was one that made us want to cut
our throats, though they didn't dare say it in so many words. A
builder of 35, a housewife of 33. A bank account that pales
against a kid's piggy bank after his First Communion. People
gave us hooded gazes. But I could feel it. I kept saying,
"Laura's still alive." What is it they say in films? A mother
knows. Well, it's true.

I knew it even when I left 167 West six months later and got
on the first train to meet a guy who used to call me a lot on the
chatline. He'd sounded like a family man; the minutes he'd
clocked up on the phone sex line paid some of the bills. He

hadn't promised castles in the air; just a meeting, no strings attached. He had been a shoulder to cry on. More than two hundred miles away, there had been someone who was willing to listen, and respond mostly with silence. Just like the man I'd married, who would come home from work red-eyed and covered in mortar. This man was more bearable than my husband, though. "You are in so much pain," he'd say. Or, "Another path awaits you." I'd ended up believing him. Not that it made any difference.

I arrived at the main train station one Wednesday with an almost empty suitcase and a cut-up expression. I wasn't walking; I was floating. We had decided on red scarves as our sign, and I'd bought a new one for the occasion, made of scratchy wool. I walked to the end of the platform and looked around. I was assaulted by the chaotic comings and goings of passersby, and the smell of fresh pastries wafting from the cafés. I'd traveled to another planet and surprised myself with a question, "What am I doing here?" The temptation to turn on my heels, head to the ticket office, and take the first train back was overwhelming. Then I heard a voice behind me. "Anna." It was different in real life. More nasal.

Antonio Romano was impressive; he had furnished a little apartment just for me. He was proud to point out all the mod cons: microwave, dishwasher, and washing machine. He'd filled the fridge. The only time he was a little ashamed was when he had to admit the view onto a dirty concrete yard was not great. That was when I asked him, "Why are you doing this?" He must have wanted something in return; I didn't believe in angels. But I wasn't scared of anything. There was no abyss anywhere in the world than could frighten me as much as the one I myself had brought into that two-room apartment, with its fresh-smelling wall units. If he'd asked me to strip right there and then, I'd have done it on the spot. Maybe that's what I'd been hoping for. That he'd exploit me. Instead, he shrugged and got a little emotional. He looked down so I wouldn't see his expression. "At least I'll be good for something," he said, handing me the keys.

Having moved from 167 West to a third-floor apartment in Milan changed nothing. The only good thing was the fact that Marco was not there. I'd loved him so much, and now just thinking about him made me want to go to the bathroom and throw up. I avoided mirrors. Catching a glimpse of Laura in my face was like rubbing salt into an open wound. Antonio Romano came every two days with supplies. We didn't say much to each other; the talk was mostly about whether the radiators were working, or some other practical issue. I used as little as I could: the same old plate, the same old glass. I went to bed fully dressed, on top of the covers. It was a way not to be caught by surprise. "Why are you doing this?" I kept asking him, while he put oranges in a fruit bowl, or tied the garbage bag before taking it out. He had stopped making comments. I couldn't have known that at that exact moment there was a man taking care of Laura in the exact same way. A man on the receiving end of the same questions.

One evening, I called home. Marco answered on the first ring. There was a long silence; listening to each other breathing. Then he put the phone down.

The months after Laura was taken away had been an ordeal for another reason too: the psychos with their mythomania, who targeted us with calls from pay phones. A voice inside me kept saying, "He knew it was me on the other end of the phone." I hated him with every fiber of my being. Rebuffing me like that, without making an effort. "You wanted to get out. Well, get out." That was it. Suffering blinds you. If he'd said,

"Please come back," it may well have not been enough. I may have dug my nails into his face if he'd shown up at the apartment where I was staying. And yet, a part of me was seeking his open arms. It revolted me to have to admit it, but he was the one who should have held on to me, tightened his grip. We'd both been crushed by the same tornado. We were both making our way through the debris. In his eyes, I had gained the upper hand, through my escape, and who knows what else. We had the same knife sunk into our ribs, but the fact that I'd abandoned him gave him the chance to be superior. "I'm staying here and facing up to reality," he'd said. It was his way of keeping our promise. To Laura. He used me, and I used him. Back then, in the depths of our misery, attempting to deal with an event that had turned our whole life upside-down from one day to the next, we were ignorant. We were imbibing the bitterness of life, without any language to express it. A limited range of measly words, which led to a limited range of measly actions. I left; he let me leave. There are cases where letting someone go is a mortal sin that marks you forever. *For ever.* A couple of weeks later, I plucked up the courage to call him again. The number was no longer listed.

Losing two people you love is no picnic. I stayed cooped up in the apartment, while Antonio Romano attempted to break down the walls of the prison that I had closed myself up in. I didn't give in. He was still a long way from gaining my trust. He was keeping me there, without asking anything in return. Hour after hour, I felt the balance owed to him growing heavier and heavier, closer and closer: "Here's your bill." There were times when I hid a knife in the sleeve of my sweater when he rang the doorbell. I carried on with my third degree: "Are you in love with me? Do you want to pimp me out?" He always looked away and asked whether I'd had any problems with the boiler. Then there was the guy upstairs who drove everyone crazy giving trumpet lessons. It sounded like a cat slaughter-house up there. One evening, Antonio Romano turned around before going out. "I lost a little girl, too," he said. Then he left.

When your kid is abducted, you try everything. There was a media frenzy with our case; stories like ours make the press merciless. They find you wherever you are. But then, your determination alone is not enough to hold their attention; without money, the flame burns out. Life goes on; there are other stories to print on the front pages. The investigation runs aground. There are no more leads to follow. Zilch and more zilch. After a few weeks, you are cut away. You curse the choices you made in the past, when nobody cared if you went to college or not. If you had done, you would have had a career by now, and your case would have had more attention. It wouldn't have dwindled to the point where it didn't merit more than a few lines in the local press. A stupid government minister opens his mouth, and you are squeezed out. The story is over. Laura's name has been added to the long list of missing children. Marco, despite the "slight problem," carries on erect-ing scaffolding, his face torn up. We can hardly keep up with the bills, never mind buy a half-page of a national newspaper. Pure fantasy. You send all your clients away. You can't bear the thought of listening to one more minute of their perverted filth. The phone sex disgusts you. So does cooking dinner. Just breathing is bad enough. The only person you still listen to is someone with the voice of a family man. He had always been an easy client, without any weird perversions, except his pen-chant for spending two hours at a time on a chat line. They're rare, but there are some clients who are only looking for com-pany. Lying fully dressed on a hotel bed, the phone calls are like an embrace. Rather than ask me what kind of panties I was wearing, this man would say, "How are you?" He wanted to chat about nothing in particular, about normal things in a normal life. Then Laura vanished. A bomb had gone off. Antonio Romano paid to listen to me cry on the phone. He paid on time. His cheques were equal to the cash-in-hand salary, plus overtime, of the builder who was now asleep on the sofa, his work clothes, stiff with dried paint, still on. The fact that I hadn't ended up blitzed out of my mind, crashing into the traffic divider on the four-lane highway at three in the morning, was all down to a stranger.

When Antonio Romano comes to visit, I call him Daddy. Still today, Daniele believes the stupid story I invented when we met: that I'd made it up with my long-lost father after almost a lifetime apart. He had been the owner of a cleaning company, and didn't have much else to his name. Except for his affair with an attractive young woman, who was my mother. A script written by fate. Daniele is fond of Daddy, but since Laura came back, he's been mad at him because he knew and didn't say anything. Now, if I look through Daniele's search history, I find my name and my daughter's instead of his home banking login. The abduction took place in '99, before the Internet became popular. There was very little information available: just two links, light-years away, after scrolling through pages and pages. Marco's accident is there, too. If you type "The Monster of the Gulf" into your search, however, the results are very different.

There are times when I stop at a café with free Wi-Fi and stare at his face. YouTube is full of his video-lectures, as well as films of his arrest, and close-ups taken before the verdict. In one video, he's taking viewers on a fascinating journey through the history of design (who would ever have thought you could say so much about an armchair); in the next, he's in handcuffs, head down, in a freeze frame from a report on his transfer. In the comments, people invoke the death penalty. In the other window he continues, galvanized by a citation: "*Is form really a purpose? Is it not, rather, the result of the process of giving form?*" With my earbuds stuck into my ears, I listen to the esteemed character, who had once been awarded the honor of receiving the keys to the town. A ceremony of great pomp and circumstance. Everyone had hailed the great man of learning. He'd been the pride of the town and, at the same time, a goad, spurring the soft underbelly of provincial life out of its infinite torpor. The presence among us of a luminary, someone who had lectured at universities all over the world, motivated us all. It was possible to make it: one of us had managed. It didn't just happen in the movies.

What made me fall in love with Milan, to begin with, was that nobody looks at you. People keep walking. Everyone is a ghost in the eyes of everyone else. Masses of people immersed in an environment where speed takes them nowhere, and yet they carry on marching, staring straight ahead. I began to understand the spirit of the city one morning when I decided to leave my little apartment and go for a walk along my street. I hadn't seen sunlight for days. It was such an unexpected gift that it dazed me, even though I was dazed most of the time back then. I still wasn't used to it. Even though Laura had been taken away, everyone carried on, going about their business. At one point, I saw a body on the ground, on the edge of a little park. It was lying facedown, arms alongside the body, palms up (which struck me), face hidden by the bushes. Blue jacket, jeans, sneakers. "Maybe he's dead," I thought. There were no bottles or syringes nearby. An old woman walked beside me, pulling a little dog on a leash. Without thinking, I pointed at the poor guy. She walked straight on. I stood there for a while, imprisoned in suspension. It was as if an energy force were aligning me with the language of the city. I felt it seeping into my blood; modifying my nature. I watched the passersby, old and young, walking along the sidewalk. Some didn't even notice; their brains didn't register anything out of the ordinary. The blow hit me when others did notice the body and simply overlooked it; it was no more interesting to them than a plastic bag, or a trodden cigarette butt. One man stopped to tie his shoelaces. A quick glance to the side, and then he stiffened, angry with himself. He'd tied the bow badly and would have to waste more precious time doing it again. Coming out of the phone booth after informing the authorities that this was where I wanted to live, I felt that this was a city of psychopaths, curated for my benefit. The only thing I desired was not to be seen.

The same is true for Laura, now. I look away from the screen and see her glide past the café window. I put some money on the counter and leave.

At first, I found it almost impossible to speak to her, but I forced myself. It was like spewing stones. I would knock on her door. "Come in," she'd say. I would open the door just a chink and show her the tray with tea and biscuits on it. She'd smile. It gave me goose bumps.

She made her way through the whole of Daniele's library. In the morning, I'd see a new gap in his bookshelves. Entertainment for the masses: detectives making the streets safe again by bringing the bad guys to justice. Laura would devour the stuff from dawn to dusk. There were no earmarks or creases in the books. No sign at all she'd read them. She'd digest them and go on to the next. "How are you?" I'd ask. "Good," she'd answer in her Martian voice.

Giving her a cell phone was traumatic: she knew how to use it.

Donà would come to our house. "It's normal," he'd say. He

would give us details, background information, keys to interpreting Laura. Day after day, he filled out the profile with
details about what they'd found in the torture room. It was like
going behind the scenes of the YouTube lectures, thanks to
which my daughter had graduated in so many subjects. When
I went into her room, she'd shake the right earbud out of her
ear by twisting her neck, and minimize the screen, or turn the
music off, with a flick of her finger. "Are you cold? Would you
like a blanket?" I would ask. Her expression said, "I spent
most of my life in an iron cage, summer and winter." But her
voice would say, "I'm fine." As soon as I closed the door, I'd
get a text message with a smiley face.

It helps me to follow her, just as it used to help me to lose
myself in the depths of the city, to understand her formulas.
Laura stops in front of the Christmas decorations in the store
windows. She slices through Milan like a poisoned shard. At
first, I thought, "She's discovering herself. She's experimenting
with distance." Then I found out she was lying. She said she'd
spent the whole afternoon at the park when she'd actually
walked ten miles without any purpose. The step counter wasn't
lying, and neither were my worn-out joints. She would sit on a
bench somewhere, music playing in her earbuds. She would
watch people go by. She took pictures of the sky, of puddles,
and buildings. Then she would let herself be swallowed up by
the subway, and resurface somewhere in the suburbs. Or she
would sneak onto a tram. It was hard work keeping up with
her. I got a sinking feeling in my stomach every time I pictured
myself in her place, standing there at some random crossroads.
I used to be exactly the same. A frayed spirit stealing down the
escalators and being thrust back up again for no reason, in a
station on the red line, fighting with the automatic doors, heart
in mouth. Sometimes, I would stop a guy on the street and ask
him the time. It helped keep my panic at bay: a face, eyes that

looked at mine, words exchanged. Other times, I'd sit in a bar, and let them get me drunk. And wake up God knows where, or with whom, feeling used.

Laura withdraws into herself. Even years later, she can't stop. It's an addiction. She may try with all her might, but there are times when she can't help it and falls back into the habit.

But first, she takes herself miles out of town. She sits in a subway car, head down. Or she closes her eyes, the music in her earbuds a buffer. She bows her head at a stop, aiming to lose every single point of reference. She takes a book out to distract herself. Then she makes up her mind, all of a sudden. She jumps up and leaps off the train, coming out onto the road and mingling with all the other lost pedestrians on the street, looking down at the road. Eventually, she picks a bar at random and shuts herself in the bathroom. She sometimes stays there more than an hour. Until someone goes and knocks—a little concerned, maybe. She often makes up a little story: the lock was stuck; she almost had a heart attack. Or she says she was feeling dizzy and fainted in the toilet for all that time. They look at her like she's a drug addict.

She does it in chemical toilets, too, or in the public conveniences at the station. It's not as satisfying, though; to find peace she needs to get lost, become an invisible dot on the map of the city. It happens at home, too. I've never told Daniele, but one morning I went to wake her up. The bed hadn't been touched. I thought Laura was in the shower (she moves around like a ghost; sometimes she appears at the door unexpectedly, and I get the shock of my life). Her clothes were all in order, folded on the back of the chair at her desk. I heard a bang coming from somewhere, and then a strange noise, like a little rodent nibbling behind the baseboard. I looked around. Eventually, I realized: my daughter was sleeping in the wardrobe.

Laura smokes. This drives me crazy, too. Before going off on her wild escapades, she stops at the tobacco store at the corner. As soon as she gets out, she rips the cellophane off the pack, pulls out a cigarette, and puts it in her mouth. She comes back in the evening after chewing a few sticks of gum on the street, but I can smell it on her breath anyway.

Apart from this, she doesn't put a foot wrong. She never skips a session with Francesca, her therapist, whom Donà had said was brilliant, a genius. She's even made a circle of friends. She's pretty; Christian, on the sixth floor, is clearly taken by her. After meeting in the elevator several times, he invited her to a party. My first comment to Daniele was, "What does she know about all that stuff?" Boys, kissing, heavy petting, and the rest of it. I wasn't asking a question. She went out beautifully made up, with a light touch. "Who taught her?" This time, I really was asking a question, but he didn't have an answer.

At night, I wake with a start, sitting up in bed. For a moment, that probably lasts seconds but feels like an eternity, I have no idea where I am or who the guy next to me in the bed is. The room is not mine. The worst bit is at the beginning: I don't even know my own name. "Laura" I hear a voice in my head saying spontaneously. Then my mind starts realigning itself, an invisible thread begins to take color, and I find my way home. By the time I sink back into my pillow, the whole picture has been filled in: my daughter is in the other room, Daniele is snoring beside me. Marco no longer exists. And I am me, the pieces of my life reassembled on the cracked canvas of a mad painter.

In my sessions with Francesca, I end up talking about myself more than about Laura. The therapist is very professional and very kind. I wonder whether she needs drugs to stay focused. She sits there behind her desk, breathing in people's darkness. Nothing throws her. She never stirs. She listens, takes notes, memorizes. "You are still living the trauma," she says. "Laura's not the only one who needs rehabilitating."

How can she speak like that about a woman whose daughter disappeared and has now returned? I should be exuberant, exploding with euphoria. Reveling in the relief of a ray of sun. And yet, here I am, living as if at the end of the corridor a black hole has suddenly appeared, sucking us all into it and holding time hostage. I feel a vibration at the back of my eyes, like when I was drinking heavily, except that I haven't emptied a bottle for years. "You must stop following her," Francesca says. "Let her go. Let her lose herself in this new world. You'll see, her 'relapses' will slowly grow fewer and farther between."

Lose herself. I had let that happen once; it was savage. Just as Marco had let me lose myself. He had opened his hands and blown the butterfly whose wings were on fire away. I look at this brilliant shrink and say, "I can't allow anything else to happen to her." The fact that really makes me sick is that maybe it's me I'm talking about. Laura takes second place. "It took me fourteen years to get over the trauma. I wasn't ready. I need to start over." In the obscene undercurrent of my conscience, there's a madwoman screaming day and night, "That daughter should never have come back." Her reappearance is a slap in the face after all the effort I have made to save myself.

Daniele is kind, but he watches her closely. Laura is not stupid; she notices and plays along, allowing herself to be X-rayed. She's clean and tidy. Perfect. After telling us about dinner with her group of friends, she ventures that she'd like a computer, a secondhand one would do. "I need it for work." What work? How come? For whom? Anyhow, Daniele ended up hauling in a pile of junk that had been gathering dust in the archive room at work for the last three years. When Laura sees it, her eyes light up with a strange yearning and she says, "Thank you."

She spends all night on the thing. I stare for hours at the bluish light emanating from under the door of her room. During the day, she goes out, walks around, locks herself in. I follow her, even though it makes me feel dirty. Once a week I go and vent with Francesca. "It's awful to say this, but the truth is that I don't trust her. There's something up." I pause for a moment and then add, "My daughter smokes." I lose the battle at the first lunge.

"Your daughter's reaction is remarkable."

I glower at her. "So, you think it's normal, do you?"

* * *

"She's sent me a friend request," I told Daniele one day. He was shocked. He knew how much it meant to me. It took me two days to click on the Confirm button.

Laura posts photos and songs. Every time there's a notification that she's posted something, I feel dizzy. She disappears for fourteen years, and when she comes back, she busies herself copying and pasting URLs. She likes bands I've never heard of. One evening, when Daniele was reading one of those books that help him fall asleep, I asked him, "Do you think it might be a code? What if Laura is sending out messages?" Expressions of paranoia of this kind are generally met by my partner's bovine expression as he tries to work out who I am. He pretends everything is normal and comforts me as much as he can. Inside, though, I can feel him pulling back. He's reeling. He no longer recognizes me. Mostly, though, he feels the stab in the ribs that is worse than all of my omissions: now he knows for sure that I'm not prepared to give him a child. My past has come knocking at the door, sweeping away all his hopes. "Good morning," Laura says when she comes into the kitchen in the morning. Sometimes Daniele answers without turning his head. "Good morning." He says it as if he were speaking to an alien.

During the years of perdition, my suffering led me to appreciate books. They didn't remedy my condition, but they did help me find words to describe the raging storm. I realized the magic of it: books make you ask big questions and contain many simple little answers. I found this out at the age of forty; what an idiot I was. Before the abduction, I was the old me: my life was panning out the only way it could for a young mother who had grown up surrounded by ignorance. Laura's return caught a very different woman by surprise; a woman who had sewn herself back together with barbed wire. To achieve this change, I'd dragged myself by the hair to libraries and museums. I couldn't be the only person in the world who had sunk down to the same depths of annihilation. It just so happened that I sensed a ray of light there. Ultimately, it kept me company. It was a temporary balm for my loneliness, which used to leave me feeling there was no escape even when I was in the middle of the crowded Galleria del Corso. I finally started lifting my head again, and I owed it to strangers who had scribbled in pen and ink, carved marble, or played the piano. By burying myself in the silence of an exhibition on the Sumerians, I gave myself a chance. I didn't look at the gold or brocade. I listened to the echoes of millennia. There was a beautifully carved hairpin, and here was me. In the middle of that bewildering array of lives lost in the rivers of time. Love affairs, deaths, adventures, and tragedies of all descriptions. An enormous waste that had nonetheless brought me there, my reflection shattering in the glass museum case, the drops of diazepam still in my system. I would go into the Fine Arts Society Permanent Exhibition and stare at a Carrà landscape for hours. Yes, me.

Laura was studying, too. But locked up in a shipping container. Donà says the education the psycho professor gave her can be interpreted in many different ways. I don't want to know any of them. The gist of it is that he manipulated her, polishing her day after day like a silver dish. Donà opens his big watery eyes wide and says, "The girl knows how to program with MS-DOS. Do you know what that means? She speaks four languages fluently." A gem. For her age, she's exceptional. She knows all about the history of populations and their migrations; she has a clear and well-informed picture of geopolitical dynamics. I look at her from the corner of my eye as she watches the evening news on TV: she stares at the screen, but she's really interpreting the news behind the news. She carefully considers every word in a head of state's speech during a visit to Qatar. She can see the hidden world that lies beneath the drama of a failing bank, which has left so many honest clients with only the clothes on their backs. My daughter, in our lawyer's books, is ready to throw herself into the world of trading.

Her treks around town are grueling. I don't have the resilience of a 22-year-old. I need rest. The house is empty, with that perfectly tidy, spotless room. There's never any need for me to go in and dust. You could perform surgery in there it's so clean. I stand at the door for a few minutes, leaning on the doorjamb. Then I make up my mind; I cross the room and walk over to the computer. Moving the mouse, the screen saver comes up—a boundless American desert. Blue sky, red boulders as old as the universe. In the middle, a box waiting for a password.

I make an attempt, but I get it wrong, again and again. During the day, I think up a list that I jot down on a piece of paper. The desert image returns after three minutes of inactivity, and I wonder, "Why does she need a password?" Laura wants to be locked inside. She needs a cell. Daniele listens to my latest rant that evening. "She could be communicating with someone." He looks doubtful. "You mean, like every other girl in the world?" he answers. This doesn't satisfy me. "What if he had given her a task?" Daniele is thrown; maybe it's not such a ridiculous idea after all. Then he downplays it, and advises me to stop. Puzzling over these fantasies isn't going to get me anywhere. We should concentrate on doing the right thing, looking ahead and not taking everything personally.

I wonder what she tells Giovanni. He's a nice kid. We often invite him in for coffee when he comes to pick her up. Daniele got along with him immediately. I observe him. Not like a mother who would keep an eye on a young man who is taking her daughter out to the movies for the first time (we all know how that ends). No, a part of me is trying to understand whether he needs to be protected. Giovanni is polite. He sometimes brings cakes. His college courses are very demanding, but he works hard. Daniele respects him a lot; he reminds him of his own youth, when he worked three jobs to pay his own way and continue his studies. I feel like sticking a gun in my mouth when he starts that old spiel. Laura comes into the living room with a smile on her face that nails you to the floor. Her boyfriend leaps to his feet. Anyone can see that he's smitten. The only thing he wants is to save up enough money to take her out to dinner. I feel myself being charmed, and I see Marco, the penniless deadbeat from so long ago with a spectacular smile. His hands were already callused at twenty. "One day, I'll take you to America," he'd say. We may have just sat down to a cheap pizza, in one of those paper-napkin places. I'd look at him, wearing my heart on my sleeve, and say, "We're there already."

The pact is to keep our secrets within the four walls of this house. Laura's arrival has turned us into improvised actors, forced us to play the role of loving relatives who have welcomed their niece, offering her room and board until she finds her way in the city where she hopes important things will happen. My daughter's performance is impressive. "Goodnight, Auntie," she says, looking me straight in the eye. Daniele can't do it; he looks away. He immerses himself in Giovanni with abnormal enthusiasm, but Giovanni seems to welcome it; it makes him feel liked. The pair go off, closing the door behind them, and the house is plunged into silence. There in front of me is the wonderful person who saved my life, but there are times when his face crumples, as if all the strength has been drained out of it. Daniele is not good at pretending, though he tries to lighten things up by proposing a fish dinner for that evening. All of a sudden, he's keen on cooking. He starts opening the doors of the kitchen units, taking out pots and pans. He opens a bottle of white wine he's been keeping aside. But even as we lift our glasses in a toast, we are unable to breathe freely.

One evening, out of the blue, I said, "Don't leave me." He didn't look surprised by my words. He may have been expecting it all this time. He smiled that smile of his, like the calm after a storm. "Don't be silly," he said, reaching out to hug me. I stopped him. "I'm begging you." I was seriously scared. He looked down. Then he said, "Tomorrow I'm taking you to Bertone's for dinner." Daniele tends to deal with any embarrassment by proposing extra courses of food. It annoyed me at first, but then I fell in love: with sitting at a table, eating and drinking (keeping ourselves alive), us. We both know the Michelin-starred restaurant is always full; every table in January has been booked since September. When I asked Daniele not to leave me that evening, he answered with a little lie.

I choose different bars, following the parabola that Laura has been tracing since she started going out. In the first few weeks, there was an invisible wall at the end of our street. She would get stuck there, keeping all her reference points in view in case she needed them to get back to her room as quickly as possible. A cockroach exploring the new house one tile at a time, after spending a month behind the sofa. Then she ventured onto the next street, and then the next. The subway stop was an important hurdle; it took a while. She used to stand there, leaning on the wall of an apartment building, watching the hordes of commuters appear and disappear up and down the escalators. In the end, she made up her mind, and allowed herself to be swallowed up. Diving into the unknown. She's still doing it now, going all the way to the end of the line. She emerges onto the street and starts exploring the suburbs. She pulls open the iron door of a seedy club with a smashed neon sign, the muffled waves of loud music coming from inside at three in the afternoon. Like me again, during those terrible years. Waiting for her at the corner of some disreputable neighborhood, where I could get knifed at any minute, destroys me. It's hard not to be noticed on those empty streets. Out she comes, safe and sound. She goes straight onto her phone to find out where she is in the city. She loves finding her way home.

Sometimes, I go in and take a look around. I may even go as far as the bar, my soul bared in my eyes. One side of me returns to being the old me, while the other is overwhelmed by the evidence that my daughter is still a prisoner. As if to justify my presence there, I go back to my old habits and order a vodka. Neat. In the middle of the afternoon. I sit at the counter, eye to eye with the barman, who takes one look at my clothes and attitude, and makes a judgment. I can see it floating like gold dust in the air: a whore who's lost her looks. It's true, in a way. With one small detail to add: that Laura is in the toilet of that sordid place. She's locked herself in to do God knows what. In my imagination, I picture her sitting on the toilet seat, buds in her ears, doing nothing. She dives into a tomb in order to get some air, so that she can free dive her way out holding her breath. When I talk to Francesca about it, she says, "How long did it take you to give up drinking?" I can't lie: it took years. In the beginning, even though I was already with Daniele, I used to keep a bottle at the back of my wardrobe. Knowing it was there gave me the strength to face the day differently. "It's the same for Laura," she says. "She'll get over it. Don't breathe down her neck."

I empty my shot glass in a hurry and go out. All I care about is that the clientele is not too rough. I'd call the police like a shot. I'd report a fight, a troublesome drunk, or my suspicion that there was some strange trading going on in the club.

The kind of people you come across in these dingy out-of-town bars in broad daylight are the same ones I used to meet: devastated dads, women kept on a short leash by jealous partners, drowning their sorrows in crates of Ceres. The worst are the middle-aged patrons who've tried everything, but would need a miracle to reinvent themselves. They're either bedraggled or in a suit and tie; either way, they're die-hards. I recognize their empty, broken gaze. Some aren't even interested in drinking. They've washed up there like old tin cans brought in by the tide and stuck in the crack of a rock from which they can't break loose. They don't talk to me; it's as if they don't see me. But the guy today attempts an approach. "Nice day," he says. That's what he says to a well-dressed woman drinking heavily at this time of day. He's clean-cut with sharp, probing eyes. Nothing like the usual patrons of places like these, who see me as a whore on her afternoon off. "Yes," I answer, looking out the window. The sky looks as though it's about to crash into the ground. Milan may well be the center of something, but from this viewpoint it doesn't look like it's going anywhere, except into a sinkhole.

"The picture," the guy insists.

"Excuse me?"

"The picture," he repeats, nodding his head at the shelves above the bottles.

It's that kitsch reproduction of dogs playing poker.

"Cute," I say, listlessly.

"Every time I look at it, it catches my attention."

I look at the discolored print. It's framed, buckling under the glass.

"Dogs playing poker. A provocation, or something like that," I say.

"*A Friend in Need*."

"Excuse me?"

"It's the title: *A Friend in Need*."

"Ah."

"The bulldog's passing the ace of clubs to his mate on the left."

"Hm."

"That's all he needs to win."

"I hadn't noticed."

"And yet . . . "

"And yet?"

"Look at the other players."

"I'm looking."

"Look closer."

"They're dogs playing poker. A provocation, or something like that."

"Seven dogs."

"Yep."

"They all have their cards covered, except the bulldog."

"Yep."

"The mate the bulldog's passing his card to under the table has the same collar as him."

"That's what it looks like."

"That's not the only thing they have in common."

"There's the aces?"

"And?"

" . . . "

"The chips?"

"They're the only ones winning."

"That's right."

"They have piles of chips, and none of the others do."

"That's right."

"The two of them are wiping out the rest of them."

"They're in it together."

"That's funny. I must have seen that picture a million times and . . . "

"*A Friend in Need.*"

"It sounds different now."

"There are two of them, the smallest dogs in the group, and they're betting for the same pot. The others might well have noticed something's going on, though. Look at their expressions."

"Yep."

"The painting captures that moment; in a second the whole thing may end in tragedy."

"The Scottish terrier gets pissed off and upsets the whole table."

"The Doberman pulls out a gun."

"A little longer and I feel like I'm at the card table with them."

"Coolidge."

"Excuse me?"

"The painter."

"Ah."

"Maybe that was his message: we're all at the same table; anything can happen."

The owner of the bar shakes his head as a bell rings behind him.

"Damn addicts . . . " he groans, heading for the bathroom.

The stranger and I climb off our stools and put our bills on the counter at the same time.

"Allow me," he says.

I run out, leaving my money there.

Daniele always said if we had a boy, he'd like to call him Igor. He doesn't talk about it anymore. Day by day, his existence is being defeated. Whereas, until a few months ago, he was the protagonist of his life, now he is just a spectator. Before, he participated in decisions, forged his own path. His words were spiced with exciting hypotheses. That is what makes life worth living. Now, he's dead. He's becalmed in the middle of a lake, adrift. "Where am I in all this?" he asks through clenched teeth after an argument. He's a pawn who has not only lost his team color, but also the chessboard. The game is being played at another table, not his. He doesn't know how to say it but, in the end, after repeated blows of my pickax, I manage to get it out of him: he's been overwhelmed by a life he hasn't chosen. Laura has been freed from her cage, but, in her turn, she has imprisoned us. The iron bars are sturdy, the prison guards control us like dogs. Daniele likes my daughter. He says, a little embarrassed, "I'm normal." There's nothing wrong with being one of the crowd, or having a life steeped in banality. He worries about Giovanni and finds our pact repellent. We're kidnapping a kid. We're not telling him the truth while he gives his all, as one does at that age. Daniele pictures him emptying the tip box and counting the coins at the end of an evening shift. "I'll use these to take Laura out somewhere," he might be saying, heedless of his upcoming landscape architecture exam. Laura is skating on a sea of ice while we are drowning in an inch of air, beneath. She's right, of course, whatever happens. Laura has paid a price that is so high it crushes us all under its weight. It would be impossible to deny her anything—if she asked for a flamethrower, we would give it to her. She's been damaged, confined. Which means she's right. She's in a weird place, and we mustn't do anything to upset her balance. Laura is a levee holding back an ocean we know nothing about. It floods regardless, carrying the boats away with it. Mine is the first to wash out to sea.

Laura is training me. After her first sprint, she sometimes slows down and gets distracted. Her phone screen an inch from her nose, like everyone her age. Milan is the perfect place for indifference of this kind. If you live there, you only see yourself; the rest is ongoing demolition. Laura looks made for the new technology: her neck is curved; her walk leaden. Her iPhone tells her what to do. She is so distracted by it that she puts her life at risk. She may take a notebook out, and jot something down. She does it suddenly, swerving to one side to lean on the wall of a building. She writes fervently, as if she has uncovered a scoop of some kind. Sometimes, she smiles. Words form on her lips, as if she is speaking to herself. Then she sets off again.

Over dinner, we try bringing up the subject of what she wants to do. Go to college, maybe? A degree may be just a piece of paper, but it's still useful. "As someone who struggled with it when I was over 30, I should know," I say. She stops eating, her gaze lost in a vanishing point. The way she suspends time like that holds your attention; it keeps you hanging. Then she resolves things in her usual manner, in one word: "travel." Coming from her, it sounds like a cannon shot. In her life she has lived in 167 West (which we've never talked about), an iron container (which we've never talked about), and in the chaos of this city. She starts eating again. Daniele makes another attempt. He picks up the ball and tries sending it back into her court. There are many jobs that involve traveling. He gives her a list of about ten. Laura listens, measuring her mouthfuls. She never reacts enthusiastically to anything.

In bed, in the dark, I say, "She's never asked about her father." For a second, it's like he hasn't heard, but then he answers, "Neither have I." A stab in the back. This is a typical technique for expressing the fact that he's out of the picture. A vertical line slicing through the comparison: long ago, there lived a man to whom I gave the thing he's asking for now. My reticence was not a walk in the park, either. Being unmasked by Laura's return shouldn't condemn me forever. He has no idea what those years were like. Daniele is as still as a marble statue. He loves me, he doesn't want to hurt me, it's just that . . . He doesn't know himself what it is. There isn't some youthful prank engraved on the other side of my coin. There's a crime that shook the entire nation.

I'm in checkmate with Laura in this, too. She knows Daddy is not my father. She was four when he was buried in the same plot as his wife. She may remember. I was overwhelmed with unexpected grief and I told her (while I was tying her pigtails before getting on the school bus to go to nursery school) that I would be lost without her. "But you are here, now," she said. I held her tight. Hugging her made me feel like she was the pillar keeping me on my feet. If I hadn't had a daughter, the grief might have cut me up into little pieces, which could have landed anywhere. Laura was there. She called me Mamma. She accepted her grandfather's death with that air of magic kids have when bad things happen. From one day to the next, the man who had spent every afternoon with her vanished into dust and was transformed into a gravestone. She had taken her first steps with him. She had spoken her first words to him. If

Laura knows how to tie a bow, it's down to my father. I would come in from my ten-hour shift at the hotel and often find them sitting on the sofa together with the TV on. She was exhausted, half-asleep before dinner. He was sitting as still and proud as the granite lions carved on the cathedral steps. Her first memories of the world were from him. He had told her the first stories, especially the ones about some of his heroic friends who'd squandered their life at the foundry: they were all artists in iron. Giant horse heads would come out of the fire, as well as the bell of the church tower and columns, which are still in place. My daughter had been entrusted to the kindest person on earth. Sometimes, they would go for a walk to the covered market, buy a slice of pizza, and eat it on the church steps. If it was raining, they'd take refuge under the portico. Laura told me about the pigeons that she fed with the last corner of her snack. There was one who limped, and she'd given him a name. Filippo, I think it was.

We were happy. Two badly paid jobs and one pension. Many people were worse off than us. Then there was the funeral. Unless you had grown up wealthy, though, there was only so long you were allowed to grieve. There was no way we could waste time being depressed on the couch. With my father's death, we had not only lost his additional income, we'd lost his presence, which was required to take care of a little girl's everyday needs. Summer was coming, and the nursery school was about to close its doors, depriving us of those few hours of freedom, which we both spent at work anyway. It would have been stupid to work all day, only to hand over my salary to a babysitter. Marco said it, "It's stupid." At least our daughter had gained a little more time with her mother.

Laura raises her hand in greeting. Daddy smiles at her. Daniele sees her distance as normal: extraneousness, the distorting effect of imprisonment. She still does it with me. Her kisses are cheek to cheek. The tall story of a father who has been allowed back into my life works for now. It would take so little for the whole house of cards to collapse and reveal one more truth to my partner—the very reason I had decided not to tell him all the rest—that I used to be a whore who sold phone sex. There's the third side of the coin.

We're all hostages. The words Laura pronounces one evening are as shocking as a shove in the dark: "I want to see our old house." Daniele looks down into his plate and stops eating. I'm about to say something like, "Let's think about it," but the words don't come out. My daughter goes on, "I'd like to go on my own."

Francesca says it's an important step: a return after forced distance. Laura needs to close the circle. "She needs it," the genius shrink proclaims. She says, "Your daughter must resolve a Gestalt." And yet, seeing her get her bag ready turns me into a wreck. At the same time, I'm the worst mother in the world. A part of me is imploring, "Go, I beg you. Give me some space." Daniele hasn't touched me for months (if we do have sex, we do it in silence, like thieves).

I advise her to take six pairs of socks; she takes two. She should fold up her sweaters and jackets; she'll only take what she's wearing. It'll just be a few days, not a lifetime. There's the beep of her phone top-up: 50 euros. I'm saying, "You never know," while my expression betrays the words, "The last time you did what you wanted, you disappeared for fourteen years."

At the door, there's embarrassment as well as a feeling of catastrophe in the air. Maybe it's how astronauts' mothers feel at their launch. Laura says, "I'll be off." She gives me an air kiss and repeats the gesture with Daniele. We stand on the doormat until the elevator comes and then we wave goodbye as the sliding doors close. My daughter disappears into an iron cage.

DOLLS

I'm telling you; I saw her. She was just outside."

"Okay."

"You don't believe me, do you?"

"What do you want to hear?"

"What kind of a question is that?"

"You keep coming back to this thing . . . "

"She was there, in the park."

"Like all the other times, you mean."

"Forget the other times."

"Okay. So, what are we supposed to do about it?"

"You don't believe me."

"I believe you. Laura was there. She was watching the house. Now, what are we supposed to do about it?"

"She was so different . . . "

"Fourteen years in that place, plus five years since she was found. Anyone would be different."

"She had a pink backpack."

"Last time, it was military green."

"Last time, it was just a girl who happened to be there."

"And today? The girl today . . . ?"

"Look, you don't believe me. I get it."

"Martina, I know it's hard."

"What's hard?"

"The whole thing, come on . . . You're living in the shadow of a ghost. I'm sick and tired of it."

"What I'm living with, is a best friend who one day vanished into thin air and didn't come back until I was about to graduate."

"Poor thing."

"Not a word in five years, not even a phone call. And this evening, there she was . . . "

"It wasn't her."

"I'm telling you it was. This time I'm sure."

"Like this summer, when you came home in tears? You'd spotted her at the supermarket. Or that other time when . . . "

"Stop it!"

"I'm just saying, you need to find a way out of this situation. You're always on the lookout, like a wary cat."

"I've looked her up on Facebook."

"What?"

"Do you know how many Laura Prestas there are?"

"No."

"A lot."

"What would she know about Facebook? Anyhow, if I were her, I'd use a nickname. She could go on as anything, for all we know."

"A while ago, she was right here in front of the house."

"Here you go again."

"She was sitting on the old swing, just like we used to do. She was looking at the house."

"Listen, Martina. This is the last time I'm going to say this. None of this was your fault."

"If I hadn't left her on her own that day, then maybe . . . "

"You need to stop this. It happened. Enough."

"She may need something."

"Well, she could ring our bell."

"How can she know I still live here, that I'm married?"

"All she needs to do is ring the doorbell."

"I saw her through the window. By the time I ran to the door, she'd gone."

"All the magazines and websites say babies feel their mothers' stress. What do you say we watch a film?"

"In the early days, I used to talk to her in the evenings."

"What do you mean?"

"I was fixated with the stupid idea that Laura could hear my thoughts. Whether she was alive or dead, I was convinced my voice would reach her, wherever she was. One day at school, they organized a whole morning session to reflect on her disappearance. There was a woman with our teacher who never stopped smiling. She gave us the shivers. A few weeks had gone by, and all our families could think about was that there must be a psychopath on the loose and that Laura was just the first on his list. Parents did everything they could to drop their kids off at the school gate before going to work. The school bus was half empty. Some mothers, including mine, took to standing outside the fence when we went out into the schoolyard for recess. Whether she'd been abducted by a maniac, or fallen into a forgotten well somewhere, didn't make much difference. Kids couldn't be left alone. I played an important role in the inquiries, having been the last person to see her or speak to her. The Carabinieri came, with some other investigators. They made me repeat our conversation on the roundabout in the park a hundred times. I had a burning feeling in my gut every time I went over our fight, which ended with me storming off in a huff. My mother nearly fainted when she heard. I'd been saved by a hair. They had to keep saying they weren't there to arrest me."

"Babe, you were a little girl . . . "

"Fourteen years later, I heard the special edition of the evening news announcing that the Monster of the Gulf had been arrested. I listened to the reports of how Laura had been found. Everyone was stunned. Like when she disappeared. Worse. The story was like something from science fiction: as if she'd been kidnapped by aliens; as if the human guinea pig had

been taken apart, put back together again, and sent back to
earth. Who knows whether she was all of a piece now? They
talked about Laura without showing her picture. After she'd
disappeared, people had made a kind of shrine there, in the
corner of our park, with a cross and bunches of flowers.
They'd left lots of little presents, but after a while it was just
me. I used to go and sweep away the dry leaves. Her mother
came a lot, too. She'd change the flowerpots and wash all the
soft toys . . . She'd sometimes find me there, and I'd give her a
hand. I still went on with that silly game of mine, though.
Talking to her. I told her about my days. As the months went
by, she faded into a funny place between memories and
dreams. This evening, she was right here outside."

"Maybe the time has come to talk to someone."

"What do you mean?"

"Listen, I don't want my kid to come out weird or anything.
Think about him. About us."

"I'll see."

"Enough with your visions, okay? Please. You're not guilty
of anything. You could look at it this way: everything has been
for the best. The psycho has been arrested. Your friend has
been freed and is starting out afresh somewhere. If she decides
to come and see us, she'll be welcome."

"There are periods when I dream about her."

"You never told me that."

"They come in waves. I turn a corner somewhere, and she's
standing there in front of me looking exactly like she did
twenty years ago. She always says the same words, without
moving her mouth: 'It's your fault.' When that bastard locked
her up, he took a piece of me with him."

"Tomorrow I'll ask around. I'll make an appointment, and
we'll go and have a good chat."

"Or I find myself there in the container. I'm her. The chain
around my neck. The whole shebang."

"We should get rid of all those newspaper clippings. Seriously."

"That day, I'd forced Laura to come out and play. She hadn't wanted to . . . "

"You're dreaming about containers and little girls accusing you of something that was out of your control. You hoard clippings like a crazy woman, and now you're coming out with this crap about seeing your friend outside . . . "

"She was there."

"And tomorrow we're going to talk to somebody."

"It was her."

"I'm begging you."

"One of the things they said was that she had a doll she called Martina. She talked to her all the time . . . So, you see, it was true she could hear me."

"Fuck."

"If only she would come and show her face. If I could talk to her, it would change everything. Even just for a minute . . . "

"Fuck."

"Listen, Andrea."

"Yes?"

"If it's a girl, I want to call her Laura."

"You want to give your daughter the name of a girl who was abducted?"

"I owe it to her. She gave my name to her doll, who kept her company for fourteen years."

"My dad will know a good therapist, for sure."

"She'd be reborn, or something like that. It's a way forward."

"We don't need anyone to be reborn. Your friend is someplace now, alive and well."

"It was just an idea."

"A sick idea. We need to get help."

"I'm fine."

"You see Laura at every street corner. I don't want a kid like that, who does weird things or who's scared of everything. The baby's living in fear; it'll leave a mark. They feel stuff inside the womb; they are being molded inside and out. I'm not inventing it. Everyone knows."

"I'm fine."

"Tell me you dreamt it."

"What?"

"Laura. The swing. The park . . . "

"I can't. She was there. I saw her with my own eyes."

"Do you want to give birth to a freak?"

"Of course not."

"A kid who refuses to get into an elevator, or shit like that?"

"Andrea, I know what I saw . . . "

"A kid with OCD, or on the spectrum? Is that what you want?"

"She'll be beautiful."

"It's a boy, for fuck's sake."

"Whatever."

"And he's not going to have the name of a ghost, right?"

"Right."

"Tomorrow, we'll go and talk with someone."

"Okay."

"Enough of this weird shit."

"Okay."

THE FEELING OF HOME

There's everything you need in the drab little hut. Drink. Books. And a laptop, open on the table. You've been staring at it for half an hour. Every minute that goes by is a point of no return. What are you going to do?

You have no idea. You're still freaked out by the wave of anger that rode over you unexpectedly. It all happened in a split second: the clang of the door, the bolts clunking into their sockets. You didn't even realize you were throwing yourself against the metal wall; it was as if another you were pulling your strings. Your heart is still beating like crazy.

It was a normal reaction. In your place, most people would have done worse things. You can tell yourself as many stories as you like, but the theft of a life still looms large. A desire for revenge is the least you can expect. And now Luca is in the cage. You've locked him up in the container just as his father did with you. The hand of the clock is counting the seconds; every tick brings you closer to the monster. But you can't unbolt the door, because he'd be right there in your face. Who knows how he's feeling about this little game? At the same time, fair is fair. He should have a taste of prison. How would the illustrious Carlo Maria Balestri see it? Being for once on the other side. It might even be useful for his son. He was looking for expiation, wasn't he? Well, here it is. You open a cupboard. There's enough food to feed an army.

You go outside. The pouring rain is pelting against the metal, making a battering noise like an army of drums. Even if you yelled at the top of your voice, nobody would hear you. You walk along the side of the brick hut and then you stop. Under your feet there's the plastic conduit for the cables going to the cage. You look at the spot where they enter the house. One second later, you're in the bedroom, dripping rain onto the tiles. You bend down over the socket, take a deep breath, and pull out the plug.

You know that an adult over 30 in good health can survive up to a week without eating or drinking. It depends on gender and basal metabolism. The main thing to avoid is dehydration, which leads to high blood pressure, dizzy spells, and hallucinations. Followed by loss of consciousness and then death. Similar to when you bleed out. Three days is a good compromise. When you unlock the door, Luca won't have the strength to run after you. That's without taking the dark into account. You remember perfectly well what happened when the door opened suddenly after days of pitch black: it felt like the light was killing you. You were blinded by it. This will also give you an advantage. You'll have to be quick, though.

You decide there and then: you'll leave the house exactly as you found it. When Luca drags himself out of the cage, he'll find everything exactly as it was. As if nothing had happened. He'll think he's been visited by an avenging ghost. He won't go far.

Why did you come? Looking back, you see your life as a road from the past to the present; in the middle there's a tunnel. Or a bridge. A massive overpass, one of those gigantic ones that disappear into the mist, where you only get back on land after driving miles in the clouds. In China there's a flyover that's 1,800 feet high. I wonder how it feels up there. Now, you're on the other side and you need to understand where you came from. 167 West, the park. Your house is inhabited by others but that doesn't matter. What matters is that it's there. It's *real*.

Your plan is simple. To weaken him: no food or water. The supplies are all in the hut; the kitchenette is clearly used. The container must be used for something else. Does he have a cell phone with him? With those walls it's useless anyway, otherwise the rescue services would already be here. He's on his own, cut off from the world. Especially in this weather. The forecast says it'll be like this for a few days.

Switching the electricity off in the container wasn't an act of gratuitous violence. There may be another computer, a Wi-Fi connection, a switchboard of some kind . . . best not risk it.

You keep the lights on in the hut. The only precaution you take is to close the shutters. You pull a flash drive out of your pocket and stick it in the laptop port, get around the password with a few taps on the keyboard, and open a blank screen. In no time at all, you're in. You start copying data.

If there's something wrong, you are unable to see it. Without the cage, you're nothing. Everyone thinks it's the other way around, but the truth is this: you've never gotten out.

Luca has his problems. But he's basically a good guy. You had him follow you around the city; once you even spoke to him. It was fun to tail him when he let you go. Giving him a sense of advantage. Feeding him with songs, pictures of roads, puddles, and skyscrapers. Standing on a street corner with his eyes on you was like an embrace. Could this be how it is to suddenly feel warm from the inside: the feeling of home? And to feel like you can't live without it?

You spend the night stretched out on the bed without taking your clothes off. When it stops raining, the dripping continues. From over there, you can hear muffled thudding, something that sounds like shouting. That's you, in the old days. You feel a throb. You might call it nostalgia.

Your mother is imprisoned in the five rooms of that apartment building, which, in its turn, is locked in the chaos of the city. You picture her desperately rifling through the shoeboxes in her wardrobe where she kept her nest egg. The absence of that money sends the message loud and clear, "You'll never see me again." You tried, but having her there in the flesh was abnormal (not to mention the lies, and that "Daddy" who was someone else entirely . . .). The image of your mother you built up over the years is more real. Or maybe the opposite is also true. There are times when distance becomes a shield, and it can't be betrayed. Once you turned the corner, the first thing you did was throw the SIM card away.

Vanish. You were taught early. A name that was swallowed into nothingness. A puff of smoke. Like you used to imagine spirits blowing down your neck when you were a little girl in your old house. They were nothing to do with death: it was just fate stroking you.

There are times when anger keeps you on the edge of your chair, your teeth clenched. The idea had been straightforward: go back to the container and decide what to do—whether to do anything—once you were there. But then you found it occupied. You have taken this transgression badly. There are moments when you are tempted to go, leaving everything as it is, with that guy in there breaking his nails on the iron walls. The more time goes by, the more you convince yourself that if there were something that had gone wrong in your life, it was the blowtorch the Carabinieri had used that day to force the container open.

The rain comes and goes. When it is calm, you are immobile; two qualities of silence competing. You don't open a faucet or turn a door handle. You know the iron isolates, but that inside you change, things happen, your senses dilate. Desperation can bring about magic. If he hasn't killed himself yet, Luca is going through the same transformation. His ears have become antennae that can hear a pin drop three hundred feet from the cabin—never mind a toilet flushing. You only move when the puddles start sloshing or when the wind shakes the willow, covering every other sound with the rustling of leaves that sounds like waves lapping the shore. It was a game you played a lot when you were in there. You used to close your eyes and imagine you were at the beach in the gulf. Now you go out of the hut and walk carefully on the grass to the door of the container. An electric shock gives you a jolt as you rest your forehead on the iron.

There's no noise coming from inside, not even whining. Then you notice the soaking piece of paper stuck through the gap at the bottom of the door. It's millimeter graph paper with writing on it you can't decipher. The letters are hard to read in the dark, and the rain doesn't help. The ink has run. You don't pick it up; you just bend down and read it. "Have fun," it says.

You know everything about him, including the *nom de guerre* he uses as a nickname on Facebook. You enjoyed watching the moves he made to approach you. He built himself quite a character. His commitment was impressive, as was his devotion to the task. What for? You asked yourself the question until you were blue in the face, but you were unable to find an answer. You could have reported him to the police: the son of the guy who locked you up for fourteen years was spending all his time stalking you. But you didn't. He goes to the same therapist, who was supposed to be helping you readjust to society. He picks up the cigarette butts you drop on the ground. He wants something. There's an ocean between feeling guilt and falling prey to the genetic seed of madness. You let the froth of the waves lap against your feet and then you walk on.

You have this advantage: Luca is convinced you know nothing about him. You even know the license plate of the car he uses when he drags himself into the city.

Maybe you should feel a little sorry for Giovanni, but when you try and think about him, nothing happens. There's not a drop of gratitude. It's awful to have to admit it, but you can't even remember what his voice sounds like. You remember his eyes. You can see those clearly: they were so exposed that one look was enough to read him. You tried as hard as you could, but breathing next to him was like being in a boring old box, with dust falling from the ceiling. You don't miss anything: not the body, not the warmth, not the tenderness. You inhabited it for a while, and that was enough. You had to find out your own way. Play the part that had suddenly been given to you. Thinking about the boy had only one effect: it made you yawn.

"Have fun." A cheap attempt. Apart from a sudden gust of wind, anyone could have locked Luca in. You checked every corner, every socket. There are no hidden cameras. Even if there were, they would be impossible to control from the container. It's fun to stir things up a little. You stick to your position. The next note reads "Hungry," with the word "Thirsty" written underneath. When you put your face close to the iron wall, you begin to smell the stench.

* * *

The days become four. There's something keeping you there. The longer you postpone freeing him, the more you risk a death on your conscience. And yet, you don't move. Everything's ready for your escape, but you're sitting on a chair, the house spick-and-span, like a mirror. There isn't a crease in the bedsheets that would betray your presence there. A joker may have passed by, or a madman hell-bent on making the family pay for the endless suffering they have caused. Or again, the father, brother, or nephew of some other little girl dumped at sea in black plastic bags decades before.

At times, it's like a curse: you're the one locked inside, even though you now have the power to unbolt the door and disappear into the woods; he's the one that's free.

In order not to leave any traces behind, you sucked on raw pasta for lunch and supper. The fruit has gone off. You have been through two bottles of water, taken from the crate that had already been opened. Luca will drag himself out of the container in a state of confusion. He won't have the clarity to take stock of what little is missing. You even allowed yourself to steal a few sips of rum. Your human waste was washed away when the heavens came to your rescue and unleashed a twenty-minute downpour. The hut is uninhabited. Repositioning the laptop precisely as you found it takes you hours. You keep on changing the inclination of the screen by millimeters at a time. Until you fall asleep on the chair, exhausted, your face on the table. When you open your eyes, midnight of the fifth day has gone by an hour ago. That's when you realize, "I'm killing him."

A Hypothesis for the Future

T he bell rings, which means recess is over. Gavin spies on Brenda Collins through the ventilation slit. She's the only one still outside, right in the middle of the field, near the swings. She's looking around. She waits one minute longer, frowning. Eventually, she mutters, "What an idiot." He chuckles to himself. She runs back into class.

Catching Mr. Parker right in front of the control cabinet was a stroke of luck. He was fiddling with the meter switches. Gavin saw him write something down and then close the door of the metal cupboard with a turn of his key. Except that the door opened again. Everyone was still playing, Sibilla Ramos counting, face to the wall. He didn't think twice.

Now his heart is beating strangely, his breath echoing and rumbling inside of him. Gavin pictures his empty desk and Mrs. Cooper fuming. His teacher hates it when they go to the bathroom right at the end of recess. Once she got angry with Brian Peterson. He rushed into class, out of breath, but it was too late. She made him stay outside a whole hour as punishment.

Five minutes have gone by since lessons started, and Gavin is thinking about this and other things. He's standing there, staring at the field through the sideways slit. There is no more yelling, just the traffic. Cody isn't a noisy town. The boy's finger is on the latch. He's about to lift it. It's time to face the music. He's about to do it, for real.

It's a kind of drowsiness.

At the school entrance he can see Mr. Parker himself. He stands there on the top step. He sweeps his eyes across the field. Then he cups his hands around his mouth and yells, "Gavin!" He mutters something and strides to the middle of the field. "Hey, Gavin!" he shouts again, this time followed by a hacking cough. He hawks up some phlegm and spits a glob onto the grass. "Fucking kids," he growls through his clenched teeth, as he starts to walk along the side wall of the building, on his way to make the rounds of the whole school.

The minutes that go by after this are fantastic; truly great. It's warm in the cabinet; the air is thick. When Gavin sees Mr. Parker pop up at the other side of the building, he almost bursts out laughing. He has to stop himself. At that very moment, Mrs. Cooper comes along. She's pretty wound up.

"Alfred?"

The janitor opens his arms and shrugs his shoulders.

"Jesus Christ," she says, running back inside.

Gavin isn't asking himself any questions. He's just looking through the slit. He knows he should leave the cabinet and bring the prank to an end. But he doesn't budge.

Mrs. Cooper is back on the warpath. There she is, at the door. Mr. Cox, in that red tracksuit he always wears, is right next to her. At Valley Elementary, the rumor is that nobody in the whole of Park County has ever seen him wearing jeans. He should win a special mention in the archives of the strangest things registered in the state of Wyoming since 1950. Mr. Cox grabs the whistle that is always hanging around his neck and blows. Then he shouts the boy's name far more loudly than the feeble janitor had managed.

When the school principal arrives, the teacher is visibly upset.

"So?" Mr. Weber asks, his face set.

She puts a hand on her chest, as if trying to catch her breath.

"Nothing," Mrs. Cooper says.

Weber takes a look around.

"He can't have gone far. The gates were closed. Let's go and check the bathrooms again, and then the changing rooms. We need to look everywhere. Mrs. Cooper, go back to your class and ask who the last person to see him was."

I'm there, just a few feet away. It's like magic. The control cabinet is so visible it's invisible. It's part of the landscape, like the plane tree or the plastic cubes the younger kids play with at recess. Anyhow, practical joke or not, any other kid in the range of fifty yards would have leapt out the first time their name was called. Gavin stands stock-still. He's inside a box. Or, everyone else has been locked out.

He has to stick his neck forward a little. It feels like the air is choking him as it goes down the curve of his throat. There are people coming and going at the school entrance. Gavin recognizes Mrs. Duchesne, the other class teacher. She flashes past and then vanishes again. The Religious Education teacher does the same. Even Miranda Boyle, the school secretary, makes a quick appearance. Usually, her only existence is there behind the glass on her swivel chair. Like a mother hen with a clutch of chicks.

Gavin can't see anything from where he is, except the field, the steps, and the school entrance, with its proud plaque commemorating Buffalo Bill (in this town, the first thing they teach you is that his real name was William Frederick Cody).

For a good while, nothing happens. It's a loaded nothingness, though. Gavin can feel the electricity in the air. It could be the meters behind him, which produce a distant background hum. He needs to pee.

A screech of brakes. A clang of the gates. Two agents walk by the sideways slit. The state troopers are here.

The boy's drowsiness is replaced by a rush of adrenaline. What is he thinking? The prank has gone too far. Before, he only had Mrs. Cooper's temper to deal with; now, there may be handcuffs. It's clear he should get out. The show's over. Gavin knows he's gone one step too far, past a special barrier. The point of no return. The news must have made the rounds of the whole school, flying from mouth to mouth, class to class. Hide-and-seek with a dramatic outcome. After today, he'll always be known as the crazy kid, who turned a prank into a tragedy just like that.

He could say he'd hidden in there and fallen asleep; that he hadn't meant to scare anyone. Coming back from a school trip to the geysers it had actually happened: they'd nearly left him at the back of the bus. He had fainted, like he'd done when they took his blood. Or been bitten by a spider. He's not crazy.

The policemen move back outside. Mr. Weber and Mrs. Cooper follow them. Brenda Collins is there, too. She looks scared; she's clinging to the teacher's skirt. They stop by the plastic cubes.

"Come on, dear," Mrs. Cooper says. "There's no need to be afraid."

Brenda points to a spot near the gates.

"Did you see your friend there?" the taller policeman asks her. He looks quite young. He's wearing those cool sunglasses with mirror lenses, like on TV.

The other one is old, his big belly stretching his uniform shirt. He walks toward the spot the girl is pointing at.

"Here?"

She nods.

"And then?"

"Then I went to hide."

Mrs. Cooper butts in.

"He can't have gotten out. The gates are always closed. You can't open them from here. Mrs. Boyle has to do it from inside. If he'd climbed over, we'd have noticed . . . Anyhow, take a look. There's no way a boy of eight could've reached that height."

The young trooper's face is blank. He takes in the teacher's words and that's it. The other one joins the group, coming into view.

"You have no idea what kids of that age can get up to . . . "

He turns to the principal.

"Have you called the parents?"

Mr. Weber clears his throat.

"Actually . . . "

"Well, the time has come to call them."

The principal looks shaken. Then he nods.

"Excuse me," he says, going back into the school.

The young trooper turns to Mrs. Cooper.

"Thanks. You can take the little girl back into class now."

She doesn't move. She just stands there, looking dazed.

"Ma'am?" the trooper insists.

Mrs. Cooper breaks down.

"I swear, he was right here. I'm not the kind of teacher who . . . "

"Calm down please. We're not accusing anyone. Take the girl back into class."

She falls silent on the spot, nodding, and takes Brenda by the hand.

"Come along, dear."

The two troopers are still there in the middle of the slit. Gavin watches them as they stand with their hands on their hips. The first one to talk is the young one.

"What do you think, George?"

George doesn't answer immediately. He stares at his shoes for a while.

"We need to tell Scott."

The young one sighs. He turns his back to his partner and leans his head to one side, speaking into the radio on his shoulder.

"Sheriff Steward, John here . . . ."

Gavin experiences the whole scene as if he were looking at himself from outside. All he needs to do is lift the metal latch, open the cabinet door, and throw himself at the mercy of one of the troopers. The old one, maybe. He could cling to his legs, or to his belt with the gun strapped onto it, crying his eyes out and begging forgiveness for his stupid prank . . . Now they're calling the sheriff. At home.

A shadow surprises him. He can see the buttons of the trooper's shirt right in front of him. Gavin pulls his head back as far as he can. Through the sideways slit, he can see the man's fingertips hammering on the heavy plastic.

"Hey, anyone in there?" the trooper calls.

Gavin holds his breath. He's saved by Mr. Weber, who tells the trooper he's called the kid's mother, and she's coming.

"What's this?"

The trooper's voice is so close, it echoes.

"The electricity enclosure."

Gavin hears a scratching noise from outside, at the height of his chest.

"The key to the cabinet?"

"It's in the secretary's office. I'll send someone to . . . "

The young trooper interrupts him.

"Scott says to carry on with our search. He's on his way." He then turns to the principal.

"How long exactly has the kid been missing?"

Weber is having a hard time.

"An hour and twenty. The girl says she saw him at the end of recess, so . . . "

The young trooper speaks to the old one.

"Scott has already sent Torczon and McClain out to patrol the area. If the kid is out of school, he can't be too far away."

The principal tries to bring them back to earth.

"I can exclude that idea completely. As Mrs. Cooper said, it's impossible . . . I mean, this is an elementary school, not a park."

He can't help himself from adding, "Visitors have to register and wear a badge . . . "

"Let's go back inside," the old trooper says. "We'll gather a team together."

The three men vanish out of view from the sideways slit. Gavin's heart is beating hard. He's thirsty and he really, really needs to pee. He's tempted to pull his pants down and do it right there. He can't. He knows what happens if you throw liquid onto electrical stuff. The whole cabin might catch fire. Now there's only one thing keeping him going: his mother. He decides he'll come out when she gets there. That way, he'll be able to dive into her arms and be safe. "It was just a joke," he'll tell her. "But then I got scared."

* * *

The screech of brakes, again. More clanging of the gates. Two plainclothes policemen cross the sideways slit. Gavin knows one by sight. It's Chris Johnson. Everyone in class knows who he is. He's an investigator. His son, Nathan, never stops boasting about his incredible escapades up and down the county. He once told them about a mysterious find, the fuselage of a spaceship or something. It was a secret, but his friend had rifled through a file his dad, who risked his life every damn day, had left lying around in his home office. Well, it turns out he's not just a buffalo hunter. He's been involved in manhunts, shoot-outs, finding bodies that have washed up on the banks of Sulphur Creek, or identifying floaters after the ice on Alkali

Lake has melted. He's fought bears, vandals, and crackpots on their way to nowhere. Now Johnson can add the kid who vanished into thin air during recess to his list of cases.

There is a commotion all of a sudden at the school entrance. The two troopers appear beside the two plainclothes investigators who've just arrived. The principal makes his way through the group and says something Gavin can't hear. Their faces are dark. Then the gates open. Weber takes a deep breath and walks down the three steps. He stops on the cement path that cuts through the field. In the sideways slit, Gavin's mother comes into sight.

"Good morning, ma'am," he says.

"Where's my son?" she asks, coming to a halt. Seeing the agents makes her knees buckle.

"We guarantee we are doing everything we can to . . . "

The woman brushes past him and strides up to the other men. "My son?"

Nathan Johnson's father speaks to her, inviting her inside.

Seeing her in that state makes the boy feel even more paralyzed. He was dreaming his mother would free him; now he feels like he's buried alive. His finger dangles over the metal latch, ready to lift it. But he can't do it. Something continues to hold him back.

Minutes go by, then the sheriff comes onto the scene. The investigator greets him and fills him in on the facts while they all walk past the ventilation slit. They disappear inside.

"Help, I'm here . . . "

For the first time, Gavin realizes he's being held prisoner. It's not his fault.

* * *

Yet again, the gate clangs. Two more agents are running across the field, holding onto their holsters with one hand and their hats with the other. They must be Torczon and McClain, the ones the trooper with the mirror sunglasses was talking about. Now they've finished the perimeter search, they're reporting back to the team.

It's hot. His legs are burning, and so is his neck. Gavin is curled up in a corner of the enclosure. There's no room to stretch out. His tummy is rumbling, too . . . The din behind him gets worse, with the noise of engines and talking. The sounds are muffled by the time they get to him: a medley of whispers, coughs, cars revving. Parents. They must be wondering what three police cars are doing in front of their kids' school. There's even the sheriff's SUV. Gavin recognizes the rumbling sound of the school bus. It's the same sound he hears every morning when it comes to pick him up at the junction of Big Horn Ave and 33rd St, in front of Joe's Auto.

It's weird to see Mrs. Duchesne at the door with all the kids in a line behind her, so quiet and well-behaved. The secretaries don't even ring the bell. There is a hush as the agents line up along the path. The gates click open. Mrs. Duchesne starts walking, and the kids follow her in pairs. It's nothing like the usual explosion after school is out. They look like deportees in a silent parade. Gavin watches the kids through the sideways slit as they approach the gate. They only pick up momentum when they see their parents and run to safety in their arms.

Kindergarten and first grade get out before everyone else. Then it's the second grade. There's Mrs. Cooper now, with the third grade. Brenda Collins is by her side. Of course, she's upset. She can't wait to go home.

The school empties out, class by class, until only Mr. Weber is left. His nose an inch away from the slit, Gavin follows the last clutches of kids leaving the school. The hubbub on the road that has been getting louder and louder suddenly stops.

"Ladies and gentlemen, it is my duty to inform you . . . "

The principal's speech is short. When they hear about the boy's disappearance, a wave of anxiety washes over the crowd as they gasp, "Oh my God," or, "That can't have happened." He even hears someone say, "Fuck." The situation is under control; Sheriff Steward is doing everything in his power. We are sure this is a prank. Things will work out for the best. Parents are requested to leave the school, so that the search can get underway. Any information may be useful; do not hesitate to contact the emergency number. If anyone wants to set up a team of volunteers, they are free to do so, as long as they obey the law and do nothing to hinder the investigation. May the Lord save us.

Gavin stares at the school entrance. His mother is there, hidden from view. The sheriff may be squeezing her a little for information, with the help of Nathan Johnson's dad. Has he been behaving strangely lately? Is he being bullied? Is everything okay at home? Can you think of any reason why he may have wanted to run away? It's often a way of getting attention.

This stuff is on TV all the time. Gavin has gotten stuck in a prank of his own making. He doesn't dare go anywhere near the metal latch in case the door opens by mistake, and they see him. When is it going to end? How? Is he going to have to stay there until the next time they come and read the meters? Mr. Parker's going to open the door one day, and the skeleton of a model pupil is going to fall into his arms, only to disintegrate into a pile of bones.

His legs are wobbly. His neck and back are both aching. He tries wriggling his toes to see if he can feel them.

The general commotion and the racket of car after car shifting into drive is fading. Eventually, after the police go back into the building, all that's left is silence. Weber has already been inside for a while.

Nightfall. That's what he has to do. Just wait until nightfall, then come out of his hiding place. The problem will be finding a way of getting over the fence without breaking a leg. Once he's done that, he'll cross town and go home. The first thing he'll say will be, "Sorry." Gavin is pretty sure that after the fright today, his mother won't punish him or have a hysterical fit. She'll vouch for him with Sheriff Steward. Then there'll be the hard bit, when she asks, "Why did you do it?" It was a dumb thing to do, everything just spun out of control . . . Inside the booth, he knows the truth is very different: "I don't know."

Most of all, what's going to happen tomorrow? Gavin imagines the moment he sticks his nose out, when the news starts spreading like wildfire: the boy has been found. No, nothing happened to him. It was just a prank. What'll it be like talking to Brenda Collins? How is he going to face every single person in the town? "That kid has a screw loose somewhere." These are the words that will brand him forever. He feels them burning on his skin already.

Maybe they'll have to leave Cody and start a normal life somewhere else.

It's certain now: the CCTV cameras on the outside of the building have not picked up any images of him hiding. They'd have found him by now if they had. Gavin's breath catches in his throat when he sees his mother come out of the school. She's a wreck. Nathan's father is all over her. It looks like he's holding her up. Sheriff Steward comes out next, with the four agents. Principal Weber, Mr. Parker, and Mrs. Boyle are the last ones out. The school secretary locks the school with a few turns of her key. They all walk off, heads down, disappearing from the sideways slit. The clang of the gates as they shut. The engines of the last cars leaving; Gavin recognizes the Nissan Altima.

Silence. The boy lets out his breath and stands there a few minutes longer. His tummy feels like a pack of wolves is running around in there. In the still silence, there's a sudden click. The door opens a chink. A clear jet of liquid forms a little puddle in the grass. Then the door quietly closes again.

It was a gamble, but he risked being fried alive if he peed inside. It feels as though the gust of fresh air has cleansed the cabinet and cleared his head. "All I need to do is stay here," he tells himself. Meanwhile, he imagines the hectic activity that must be going on in town: good family men giving up paid work to join the search party; citizens patrolling the area in their pickups; groups combing through every neighborhood, scouring the other side of Spring Creek, even. They're probably discussing the worst possible scenario: an abduction. Gavin imagines the sheriff asking his mother whether there's anyone who means them harm. Anyone who might do something like this. In the movies, it's usually about money or revenge of some kind. "Ma'am? Is there any possible explanation of any kind?" They'll ask to speak to her husband, too. Except he's not there.

He comes once a week nowadays, usually on Sundays, to spend time with his kid. Gavin thinks that his kid disappearing must be important enough for him to be on the road now, his foot flat on the gas. From the enclosed space of the booth, he sees that evening flash. He was pretending to be totally into a videogame with his headphones on at full volume but, actually, he'd turned the sound down. He suddenly wonders, "Could a kid disappearing bring two parents together who can no longer stand to look one another in the eye?"

He has never understood a thing. The fact is that, since that fight, nothing has been the same. At the end of the argument, the front door had slammed, and his father had disappeared.

Gavin pictures himself playing *Total Invasion 8*, his team of rebels penetrating the arid, perilous lands of Golma, a planet in the seventh solar system of Hagart. It's his favorite war game, especially because the captain's aide-de-camp is called Jason Wood, just like his father. He's a mercenary intergalactic fighter with a mechanical arm that can pulverize mountains and that can transform itself into a photonic cannon, if necessary. Gavin never chooses him; he prefers war gaming as Ulto Bear and watching Jason Wood from the captain's perspective. Of all the rebels who throw themselves into the battle, they are almost always the last two combatants left standing.

As well as having his volume on zero, there's the advantage of the French windows. From the reflection in the glass, Gavin can see what's going on a few feet away, past the arch, in the kitchen.

It isn't a normal fight; that's clear from the start. For one thing, they're speaking Italian, which only happens rarely. It's a language that's full of sharp edges. He only speaks a few words of it but on days when he's feeling in form, he can put together a few basic sentences—though his mother's always criticizing his grammar.

They've tried telling him about their old life on the other side of the world, occasionally: the cities they'd lived in, what they'd studied . . . Then their first meeting, which soon led to them getting married. One day, they said, they decided to do something crazy: they dropped everything and crossed the ocean to invent a new life for themselves there. His mother looked at him. "It all started again with you," she said, her eyes brimming with love. These words were supposed to be nice, but Gavin felt the weight of them on his shoulders; they were a millstone he didn't need. To change the subject, he started bugging her to name things in Italian: table, coatrack, living room, lampshade . . . He loved listening to her in another language. His mother obliges him for a while but then she always pulls the plug on the game. There's always something she needs to do, right there and then. There's no point in badgering her any more. It doesn't happen often, but there are times when he digs his heels in, when he has the feeling that they don't want to include him in the story even though he is part of it. "Stay in your place," is what he feels they're telling him when he insists on knowing stuff, or asks too many questions. Together, they burdened him with the responsibility: "It all started with you." Gavin knows he has no family except them. He's not the only one in his class, though; Gordon Seller, for example, is the same (people think that's why he's a bully). Gavin knows the town of Cody like the back of his hand. Outside Park County, though, the landscape is a fog.

The fight in the kitchen is about Sarah Hawkins, the woman on Sheridan Avenue who makes a mint selling over-priced fridge magnets and postcards. Tourists on their way to or from Yellowstone spend a fortune without batting an eye. Among the best-selling items is, of course, Buffalo Bill. There is a brisk trade in miniatures of the local hero. Gavin's father no sooner delivers the new models than the window display is ransacked. He's a genius. He spends most of his day in the workshop at the back of the house. It's like stepping into another world: shelves and shelves of characters. Gavin sometimes gets permission to pick one up. He takes it to the work-top and puts on the special glasses his father uses to model the mini putty figures. The lenses magnify the details: the clothes, buckles, and pelts . . . He can be mesmerized by a wooden button for a quarter of an hour without knowing why. His father has hands of gold. With his tools and brushes he sculpts unique collectible soldiers by hand. He gets orders on the Internet every day. His miniatures are sent from Cody around the world. There are families willing to pay half a month's salary to be immortalized. They just need to send a photo.

On the mantelpiece over the fireplace, there are models of his own family: father, mother, and son. It's time to celebrate when, once a year, Gavin gets to follow the process from beginning to end, with bated breath, staring at the putty mix. "Giving form outside is giving it inside," his father often mutters like a mantra while he's working. At times, he's sure it's true; other times, he thinks it's stupid.

This happens at Christmas; it's become a tradition. The Wood family is sculpted in every transformation, from him in a pram to him standing up, and so on. Each tableau sits in the living room until the following December, when the new one comes along. It's funny to see all the transformations lined up on the shelf in the workshop. The first set features just his mother and father. She's pregnant. On the pedestal are carved the words "Wood Family, 2019." Gavin often pauses in front of these two mini figures. He feels as though he's made of smoke. A hypothesis for the future that has not yet been born.

"Were you following me?" he asks. Gavin has the impression his father almost enjoys the idea of being tailed.

His wife is not in the mood for jokes.

"Fuck off," she says angrily, clenching her teeth.

"Come on. Let's not make a scene. What came over you, I wonder?"

"I saw the two of you. There. In the back storeroom. You disgust me."

He's serious now.

"You followed me," he repeats, this time as if he were thinking out loud. Then he must realize the seriousness of the situation and looks shaken.

"I don't know what you saw, but with Sarah . . . "

"You disgust me," she says again. She looks as though she's about to faint and has to grab a chair.

"We fucking had everything . . . How could you?"

Gavin is at a delicate moment in the game: Ulto Bear is guiding his team of rebels through a minefield; he needs to keep the winged mutants flitting around in sight. It takes skill. He knows the solution is a double somersault and a green bomb just as the hero is at the top of his flight. The giant insects are smashed to smithereens and the intergalactic pirates find a gateway through the chaos.

"Do you love her?" she asks.

"Don't be stupid."

"So, why?"

Gavin's father lowers his head.

His mother is devastated.

"How could you?"

Every time she says this, it looks like her head is spinning so badly she needs to lean on the sink. He looks like an iron mask. He's looking down in silence.

"Say something . . . speak!" she shouts but he doesn't say a word.

After insisting repeatedly with no result, she goes off her head and runs out of the kitchen. Gavin sits for a few minutes guiding his army and observing his father in the reflection, staring at his hands. Then she shoots back, like a torpedo. She places a clipping she's found someplace in the middle of the table. All of a sudden, whatever happened with Sarah Hawkins becomes irrelevant.

Locked in the cabinet, Gavin asks himself the same question he asked that evening: how can a newspaper clipping wreak such havoc? He may have been unleashing Ulto Bear against giant worms with carapaces of steel, but inside he was as cold as marble. He's never seen his father like that. He starts to cry. The boy feels a burning sensation. A special move: Jason Wood's club catches fire, exterminating monsters that fill the screen. But he's missed something: his hero hasn't noticed the mutant attacking the army from a rock on the left. A house on Big Horn Avenue detaches itself from its foundations, and lands on Golma.

His mother stares at the table. She suddenly looks sorry for showing him the clipping, as if she were waking up from a dream. As if it had been an expression of anger she would happily have taken back. Her eyes seem to be saying, "Oh my God, what have I done now?" Or maybe this little revenge was just waiting to happen.

His father's face is crumpled. He's mumbling words that make no sense.

"You know."

There's no going back for her. Her answer is silence.

He needs to catch his breath. He's reading a story—or something—in that clipping.

"You needed me," he says, eventually. It looks like he's guessed the only answer that would solve the puzzle. "You weren't looking for me; you were looking for my father. You just wanted to get back into that fucking container . . . "

"The only thing *you* wanted was to get me back in there. You had to save me. Wash your father's blood off your hands. There's nothing you can do. You're just like him."

"You took my name. I gave you a new start, on the other side of the world."

"I gave you a son. You wanted to be born again, away from everything, didn't you?"

He looks wild-eyed. He's taken over by fits of hysterical laughter.

"Who locked up who?"

They can't look each other in the eye.

Gavin's memories fade into a vortex of alien words. He sees himself there with his controller in his hand, the game counter inexorably running down to zero. His parents don't notice him. They're just spitting horrible things at each other. Like his father saying the town of Cody is a "cage." An urn with invisible walls, miles away from the rest of the world. Enough to drive you crazy. Or like him saying they're locked inside themselves. That it's one thing keeping each other company and living side by side, but it's another matter altogether checking up on each other, living in each other's shadow. Two solitudes don't make you free. The only thing you need to change is the way you see your prison. You start to have no air anyway, and you look for cracks, gaps, slits . . . A hug from someone like Sarah Hawkins can give you a little breathing space. Some of the phrases he heard that night continue to buzz around in Gavin's head like a swarm of flies whizzing past at a thousand miles an hour.

"We sought each other out," his father says, still looking at his hands. "At the end of the day, I can only say it was fate. I really do love you. Things had to go all that absurd way to. . ."

She shakes her head, not giving him an inch.

"We used one another."

For Gavin's father, this is the fatal blow. Seeing the clipping seems to have erased him from the face of the earth. He gets up and storms into the bedroom, disappearing from view. His mother follows. She's not done with him yet. Only then does Gavin take his headphones off and rest his controller on the sofa.

He can hear muffled bangs coming from the other room, drawers being opened and shut angrily. He gets up and goes through the arch into the kitchen. He leans over the table. There's a newspaper clipping, yellowing at the corners, with faded print. He has no idea what's written there. In the middle of the article there's a photo of a little girl. The only word he recognizes is the name written in block letters under the picture: LAURA. Like his mother.

* * *

The light has changed outside. Gavin gazes out at the field through the ventilation slit, but what he's really staring at is the little girl's face. Sometimes, he dreams about her. They are nightmares he wakes up from drenched in sweat; all of a sudden, the black-and-white image starts to speak, in words he can't understand. They might be able to explain why he is here now, with the whole town of Cody coming after him following a moment of madness that has nailed him down to this spot inside the control cabinet.

For a while now, hunger has taken on a different quality. He's never felt like this before; now he knows how bears feel in the winter, when they come out of the woods and brave the town streets to rummage in the garbage. Thirst, too. Gavin can't tell where one starts and the other ends. And yet, all he needs to do is lift the metal latch and open the door. Stand in front of the big solid fence surrounding the school, and yell. Somewhere, inside of him, he's already doing it, closed in the cabinet. Until a thought flashes through his mind all of a sudden. It's the only glimmer of light and he clings to it with all his strength. It's like turning the whole world upside-down.

"Let's see what they'll do," he says to himself.

ABOUT THE AUTHOR

Sacha Naspini, born in Grosseto in 1976, is an editor, art director and screen writer, and the author of several novels and short stories.